OLD CELTIC TALES

Start Publishing PD LLC
Copyright © 2025 by Start Publishing PD LLC

Start Publishing PD is a registered trademark
of Start Publishing PD LLC
Manufactured in the United States of America

Cover Art: Stockcake
Cover Design: Paula Guran

ISBN 979-8-8809-2585-8

OLD CELTIC TALES

E. M. WILMOT-BUXTON

THE CHILDREN OF LIR

Lir, a powerful Irish chieftain, had married the eldest of three beautiful maidens, and in course of time they had four fair children—a daughter and three sons. Sad to say, the mother died when they were still very young; and Lir married again. His new wife, who was named Eva, was also very beautiful, but, though no one knew it, she was a very wicked sorceress. She could not bear to see her husband go to fondle and play with his children, and at last she determined to do away with them altogether. So one day she enticed them to a lonely spot among the mountains, near a smooth lake, and, leaving them to play together, she tried to bribe her servants to put them to death. But they would not, and so she returned to them determined to do the deed herself. Now, when she reached the spot, and saw how fair they looked as they ran races about the valley, her heart failed her, and she could not do this wicked thing. But she was determined that they should not return to their father Lir, so she called to her an ancient Druid who lived in a cave near that spot, and persuaded him to use his enchantment to obtain her wish. When the Druid had advised her what to do, she called the little ones to her, and said to them: "Children dear, how warm you are with your running! Come and let me bathe you in Lake Dairbreak, that you may be cool and refreshed."

The children were delighted to do so, and were soon splashing about in the clear water, but no sooner had the water covered them than by the magic spells of Eva and the Druid they were all four changed into swans.

"Birds shall ye be," chanted the Druid from the bank as the change took place, "until, long ages hence, ye hear the voice of a Christian bell."

So the four beautiful milk-white swans swam sadly away over the smooth water; and when the cruel Eva saw what she had done, she feared to face her husband, and repented bitterly of her evil deed. But it was too late. All she could do was to grant to the birds the use of their native speech, their human reason, and the power of singing plaintive fairy music, so sweet that those who heard it should be soothed and calmed, however sad and angry they had been before.

A terrible punishment overtook their wicked persecutor. When the King of that country heard of her cruel deed, he sent for her, and asked: "What shape of all others on the earth, or below the earth, or over the earth, do you most abhor?" She replied: "A demon of the air."

Then the King pronounced judgment on her: "A demon of the air shalt thou be till the end of time."

Meantime hundreds of years passed away, and still the beautiful swans swam up and down their lake and looked for deliverance. Sometimes they took flight, and entered the Western Sea, and sailed around the coast; but all Ireland was in heathen darkness, and never the sound of a Christian bell was heard.

The dwellers of those coast lands used to visit the shore in crowds to hear their sweet music and watch their graceful movements. But after a time they were caught by the strong current of Mull, and this drove the fair birds into the stormy seas between Erin and Alba. Here they endured many a woe; for sometimes they were separated from one another by the storm and darkness, and sometimes they were almost frozen to death in the icy floods. And so, tormented by the restless waves and the chill winds of winter, they waited for three hundred years. But one soft spring morning, when the ice-floes had drifted away and the wind sang gently over the mountains, as they floated along their own Lake Dairbreak, they heard the sound of a Christian bell. For St Patrick had come to Ireland with the glad Gospel news, and everywhere men were building churches, and hastening to fill them with worshippers.

So when the sound of the distant bell floated over the water, the spell was broken, and the Children of Lir returned to their own shapes. But they had lived so long that, after they had learnt the Christian faith, they were glad to lie down and rest for ever. They were all buried in the self-same tomb, and after their death men made songs about them; and every Irish boy and girl to this day loves to hear the story of the Swan-Children of Lir.

From the earliest mythological cycle of Celtic poems. No copy of it is found in writing till the early seventeenth century.

THE QUEST OF THE SEVEN CHAMPIONS

I. The Seven Champions of Arthur

These stories were told in old days to British boys and girls as they sat round the fireside and heard the wind outside skirling among the wild Welsh hills. But, no doubt, in time they crossed the border, and were told also to English children, such as most of you, who knew and loved the charming tales of Arthur and his knights.

In the days of King Arthur there lived a noble young prince named Kilhugh, to whom it had been foretold that he should never marry until he could win for his wife the maiden Olwen, daughter of Thornogre Thistlehair, the Chief of the Giants. But, though he was full of love towards the very name of the unknown maid, he could not find out where she lived, nor could anyone tell him anything about her.

He was not cast down, however, but set off upon his steed of dappled grey to seek help from his kinsman Arthur. A fine sight he was, indeed, as he rode along on his prancing horse. His bridle was made of golden chains, his saddle-cloth of fine purple, from the corners of which hung four golden apples of great value.

His slung war horn was of ivory, his sword of gold, inlaid with a cross that shone like the lightning of heaven; his stirrups also were of pure gold. Two spears with silver shafts were in his hand, and two beautiful greyhounds, wearing collars set with rubies, sprang before him "like two sea-swallows sporting." So lightly did his charger step that the blades of grass did not bend beneath his tread.

At length he came to Arthur's castle, and having with much difficulty satisfied the Chief of the Porters of the Gate, a sturdy warrior known as the Dusky Hero with the Mighty Grasp, he made his way into Arthur's presence, and told the King his story.

"This one boon I crave of thee, O King," he ended, "that thou wilt obtain for me Olwen, the daughter of Thornogre Thistlehair, Chief of the Giants, to be my bride. I ask it of thee and of all thy valiant knights, for the sake of all the fair ladies who have ever lived in this land."

Then Arthur said: "My Prince, I have never heard of this maiden, nor of her kindred, but messengers shall at once set forth to seek her if thou wilt give them time."

So it was agreed that, this being New Year's Day, they should be given until the last day of the year for their quest.

The messengers of Arthur set forth in haste, each taking a different way. They travelled throughout all the land of Britain, the "Island of the Mighty," and then to foreign lands, asking as they went: "Dost thou know aught of Olwen, the daughter of Thornogre Thistlehair, Chief of the Giants?"

But everyone said "No."

At length came the end of the year, and on the appointed day the messengers appeared in the wide White Hall of Arthur's castle, and all alike declared that they had no news whatever to declare concerning the maiden Olwen.

Then Kilhugh was very angry, and said in hasty words: "I alone am denied by my lord the gift I ask. I will depart from hence at once, and take with me the honour of Arthur, whom men call the most honourable King." But Kai, one of the knights, reproved him for his angry speech, and offered to go forth with him and any others who would accompany them, saying:

"We will not part till we have found the maiden, or till thou art forced to own she is not among those who dwell on this earth."

So Arthur chose six of his knights to go forth with Prince Kilhugh upon his quest.

First came Kai, whose offer had but just been spoken. An excellent spy and sentinel was he, for he could make himself as tall as the tallest tree in the forest, and so scan all the country round. He could hide himself under water, and lie hidden in lake or river for nine days and nights if need be. Such fire was in his nature that when they needed warmth his companions had but to kindle the piled wood at his finger; he could walk through torrents of rain as dry as on a summer's day; he could go for nine days and nights without sleep, and no doctor could heal the wound made by his sword.

Next came Sir Bedivere, close brother-in-arms to Kai, the swiftest runner, save Arthur himself and one other, in all the land. One-handed was he, yet he could give more wounds in battle than any three warriors together.

Then followed Uriel, who understood the speech of all men and all beasts; and Gawain, who was called the "Hawk of May," because he never returned from any undertaking until it had been performed by him.

The fifth to answer Arthur's call was Merlin, a master of magic, who knew how to put a spell upon the knights that would render them invisible.

Last came Peregrine the Guide, who knew how to find the way as well in a strange country as in his own.

"Go forth, O Chieftains," said the King, "and follow the Prince upon this quest; and great shall be the fame of your adventure."

So the Seven Champions rode forth through the great gates of the palace, and set out with high hearts to seek for Olwen, daughter of Thornogre Thistle-hair, Chief of the Giants.

II. How the Seven Champions found Olwen of the White Footprints

Onward and onward rode Kilhugh and the six knights until they came at length to a vast plain, stretching in every direction farther than the eye could reach. Over it they rode, and at length perceived through the misty air the towers and battlements of a great castle far away on the borders of the moorland. They rode towards this castle all day long, but yet they never seemed to get any nearer.

All the next day they went on riding, and still the castle seemed as far away as ever. The third evening brought them no nearer. At length Sir Gawain exclaimed: "This must be Fleeting Castle, which can always be seen from a distance, but can never be actually reached."

Now, on the fourth day, to their surprise, the castle no longer advanced before them as they approached, and soon they were able to draw rein before it, and to wonder in amazement at the thousands of sheep which fed upon the plains surrounding its massive walls. Near by sat the shepherd with his dog, tending this enormous flock. The shepherd was a giant in size, and was dressed in the skins of wild beasts. The dog was larger than a full-grown horse; he had the shaggiest of coats, and, though an excellent sheep-dog, was destructive enough elsewhere, for with his fiery breath he would burn up all the dry bushes and dead trees in that region.

The Champions looked somewhat doubtfully at this great animal, and Kai suggested to Uriel that as he knew all tongues, he had better go and speak to the shepherd.

"Not I," answered Uriel. "I agreed when we set out to go just as far as thou, and no farther."

But Merlin came to them, and explained that he had cast a spell over the dog, so that he could not hurt them. So Kilhugh and Kai and Uriel went together to the shepherd, and asked him very politely who owned that countless flock of sheep, and who lived in yonder castle.

"Where have ye lived not to know that?" cried the shepherd. "Everyone in the world ought to know that this is the Castle of Thornogre Thistlehair, Chief of the Giants."

"And who art thou?" they asked.

"I am Constantine, the brother of Thorn ogre Thistlehair," replied the man, with an angry look. "A fine brother indeed has he been to me! He has taken from me all my lands and possessions, and now I am obliged to earn a living by feeding his sheep."

Then he asked them why they came, and when they replied that they were seeking for Olwen, daughter of Thornogre Thistlehair, he sadly shook his head.

"Alas!" he said, "no one ever tried to find her and returned from this place alive. Go back at once, lest ye all perish also."

"That will we never do!" cried Kilhugh; and the Champions echoed his words.

Then Constantine inquired who Kilhugh was, and when he heard, he cried out that he was his own nephew, and begged that he and his comrades would spend a night at his house, and to this they readily agreed. And as a mark of affection Kilhugh gave his uncle a golden ring; but it was much too small for the giant, who put it forthwith into the finger of one of the gloves which hung from his belt as a sign of his rank as chieftain. Then he signalled to his dog, who immediately began to drive the sheep towards home.

When they reached the house the giant entered first, and gave his wife his gloves to hold. She soon pulled out the ring, and at once began to question him about it; so he told her that their nephew Kilhugh, with six comrades, was even then dismounting at the door. Then the shepherd's wife was glad, and ran forth with hands outstretched to clasp him in her arms; but so big and strong was she that, as Kai quickly saw, no knight could survive her embrace. So as she threw her arms round Kilhugh's neck, he snatched up a log of firewood, and pushed it into her arms instead of the young prince; and when she unloosed it, it was twisted out of all shape. It was somewhat to their relief, therefore, when she took them into the house without further embracing, and set them down to supper. This was a very frugal meal, and served with great simplicity, for Thornogre had not left his brother so much as a silver goblet or a single chair in his barren hall.

When they had supped, the shepherd's wife asked Kai and Uriel to stay behind after the rest had gone out to the courtyard, and, taking them to the chimney-corner, she opened a great stone box. As she lifted the lid, to their amazement a beautiful boy with golden, curly hair rose up from within.

"Pity indeed," exclaimed Uriel, "to keep so handsome a child shut up here. What hath he done?"

Then the lady wept, and answered: "All my three and twenty sons have been killed by Thornogre Thistlehair, Chief of the Giants; and now my only hope of keeping him alive is to hide him in this chest, where he has lived ever since he was born." And she wept to think that her boy would never have a chance of doing valiant deeds and of becoming a great knight. Then Kai bade her be of good cheer and let the lad come with them, promising that he should not be slain unless he, Kai, were killed as well.

She agreed to this very gladly, and asked them why they had come to that region. But when she knew they had come to seek for Olwen, she advised them strongly to go home, since in that very quest all her three and twenty sons had perished.

They laughed at her fears, however, and asked if the maiden ever came to the shepherd's house.

"Yes," said the shepherd's wife; "she comes every Saturday to wash her hair. She leaves behind her all her jewels and rings in the water which she uses, and never asks for them again."

Then they begged her to ask fair Olwen to visit her at once, and she agreed, on condition that they would not carry her off against her will.

To this the Champions agreed, and sat waiting in a hall for the coming of the maiden.

Very fair she looked as she approached, dressed in a robe of flame-coloured silk, and wearing a jewelled collar of gold round her neck.

More yellow was her hair than the flower of the broom, and her skin was whiter than the foam of the wave; and fairer were her hands and fingers than the blossoms of the wood-anemone amidst the spray of the meadow fountain. The eye of the trained hawk, the glance of the falcon were not brighter than hers. Her bosom was more snowy than the breast of the white swan; her cheek was redder than the reddest roses. Whoso beheld her was filled with love of her. Four white trefoils sprang up wherever she trod; therefore was she called Olwen of the White Footprints.

Having entered the house she sat down by Kilhugh, who at once loved her greatly, and began to pray her to come away with him, and be his wife. But Olwen, though she returned his affection, answered that she had promised her father not to go away without his leave. She also told him that Thornogre knew that her bridal day was fated to be the day of his death, so that he would with-hold his leave as long as possible. She advised him, however, to go to her father, and to grant him everything he demanded, and so in time he should win her hand; but if he denied the giant's least request, he would lose both her and his own life.

When she had said this, she returned to the castle.

III. The Impossible Tasks set by Thornogre Thistlehair

The Seven Champions now determined to make their way to the castle, and force an entrance to the hall of Thornogre Thistlehair, Chief of the Giants. It was very dark when they set out, but they easily found their way by the trail of white trefoils which the footprints of Olwen had left.

The castle was guarded by nine warders at the gate and nine watch-dogs along the road which led up to it; but a strange silence had fallen upon both men and beasts, and the Champions slew them all without a sound being heard.

Then they passed through the great door, and entered the hall of the castle.

Just opposite the entrance sat Thornogre Thistlehair upon a high, wide throne. He was terrible to look upon. His eyebrows were so long and bushy that they fell over his eyes like a curtain, and he was taller and broader than three other giants put together. Close by his hand lay three poisoned darts.

After they had greeted him courteously, he asked who they were; and they replied that they were come from Arthur's Court to ask that Olwen, his daughter, should marry Kilhugh the Prince. Then the giant roared for his pages to come and prop up his eyebrows, that he might see what sort of son-in-law was proposed for him.

So when they had propped up his eyebrows he looked angrily at Kilhugh, and bade him come the next day for his answer.

But as they went out of the hall, the giant threw one of his poisoned darts at them. Sir Bedivere caught it just in time and threw it back so neatly that it caught the giant in the knee. Then they laughed, and withdrew, leaving him to storm at them, declaring that the great wound hurt him as much as the sting of a gadfly, and that he might never be able to walk quite so well again.

At dawn the next day they returned to the castle, and again demanded the hand of fair Olwen in marriage. But the giant replied: "I can do naught in this matter till I have consulted her four great-grandmothers and her four great-grandfathers. Come again for my answer."

So they turned to leave the hall; but as they went the giant snatched up the second of his poisoned darts, and flung it after them. Merlin caught it deftly, however, and threw it back with such force that it entered his chest, and stuck out through his back. This left him grumbling that never again would he be able to climb a hill without losing breath, and fearing lest he now might sometimes suffer from pains in the chest.

The third time they visited the giant he was on his guard, and shouted to them not to dare throw any more darts on pain of death. Then he roared to his pages to lift up his eyebrows, and when they had done it, he snatched up the third poisoned dart, and flung it at them without more ado.

But Kilhugh caught it this time, and cast it back at him, so that it pierced one of his eyes. Then, while he grumbled that now his sight would not be so good as before, they went out to dine.

These events made the giant treat his visitors on their next arrival with more civility; besides, he had no more poisoned darts. He once more inquired why they had come, and when he realised that Kilhugh was determined to marry Olwen, he made him promise that he would do all that he required of him in return for his agreement to the marriage. Kilhugh, mindful of Olwen's warning that he was to agree to perform whatever her father proposed, gave a ready promise, and bade him ask away.

Then did Thornogre Thistlehair propound to him forty Impossible Things, of which these seven are the chief:

Firstly, he must gather nine bushels of flax sown hundreds of years ago in a field of red earth, of which never a seed had sprouted. Not one grain of the measure must be missing, and they must be sown again in a freshly ploughed field to make flax for Olwen's wedding veil.

Secondly, he must find Mabon, the son of Modron, who was stolen from his mother when three days old, and had not since been heard of.

Thirdly, he must find the Cauldron of Cruseward the Cauldron-Keeper, in which, if one tries to cook food for a coward, one may wait for ever for the water to boil, but if for a brave man the meal is ready directly it is placed therein. In this cauldron must all the food for the wedding feast be prepared.

Fourthly, since the giant must shave for the wedding, he must obtain for a razor the tusk of the Boar-headed Branch-breaker, which to be of any use must be taken from his skull while he yet lived.

Fifthly, since the giant must wash his hair, all matted together as it was, for the wedding, he must bring to him the Charmed Balsam kept by the Jet-Black Sorceress, daughter of the Snow-White Sorceress, from the Source of the Brook of Sorrow, at the edge of the Twilight Land.

Sixthly, that the giant's hair might be smoothed and combed he must bring the scissors and the comb that are found between the ears of Burstingboar, the Wide-Waster, since they alone would perform the operation without breaking.

Seventhly, he must obtain the sword of Garnard the Giant, since that alone would kill the Wide-Waster, from whom, unless he were killed, the comb and scissors could never be obtained.

When he had made an end of speaking, the giant jeered at the Prince, who, unless he could do all these impossible things, might never wed his daughter. But Kilhugh answered with a high heart: "I have knights for my companions, horses and hounds, and Arthur is my kinsman. I shall do all that thou requirest, thou wicked giant, and shall win thy daughter, but thou shalt lose thy life."

IV. Two of the Impossible Tasks are fulfilled

Scarcely had the Seven Champions left the castle of Thornogre Thistlehair when they were joined by the fair-haired son of the shepherd, who had lived all his life in the chest. Eager to make a great name for himself he implored them to let him accompany them, which accordingly they did. Then they turned their faces towards Arthur's castle.

At evening-time they reached the gates of a very great castle, the largest in the world, and as they pulled up their horses before it, an enormous black giant came out of the gate, and looked at them very hard. They greeted him politely, and asked whose castle this was.

"'Tis the castle of Garnard the Giant," he answered.

They looked at each other with glee, for one of the appointed tasks was to obtain the sword of this very giant. Then they asked if he were used to treat strangers courteously.

The black man shook his head. "No stranger ever entered that castle and came out alive," said he; "but ye have little chance of entrance, for no traveller is permitted to enter who knows no handicraft."

The Seven Champions on hearing this rode on to the entrance gate, and called for admittance. The porter refused, however, saying that there was revelry within, and that no man set foot inside who did not bring his craft with him. But Kai declared that he was a burnisher of swords, and that no man could excel him at that trade, whereupon the porter went to report the matter to Garnard the Giant. Now, it so happened that Garnard had long wished for one who could brighten and clean his sword, so he bade the porter to admit him.

So Kai entered alone, and was brought before the giant, who ordered his sword to be brought to him. Then Kai drew out his whetstone, and, first asking if he required it to glitter with a blue or a white lustre, he polished half the blade, and returned it to the giant, saying: "How is that?"

The giant was highly pleased. "If the rest of my sword can be made to look like that," said he, "I shall value it above all my treasures. But how comes it that so clever a craftsman is wandering about alone without a companion?"

"But I have a companion," said Kai—"a cunning craftsman, too, though not at this work. Send, I pray you, and admit him. And the porter shall know him by this sign: the head of his lance shall spring into the air, draw blood from the wind, and return to its place again."

Then the porter opened the gate, and Bedivere marched into the hall, ready for what might befall, and stood watching Kai as he went on polishing the sword. This being done, to gain more time he asked for the sheath, and he fell to mending it and putting in new sides of wood.

Meantime, as he had hoped, while all the porters and followers of the giant stood gaping round him, the young son of the herdsman had managed to climb over the castle wall, and to help his companions over also, whereupon they were able to make their way to hiding-places behind doors and pillars, from which they could see the company in the hall without being seen themselves.

By this time Kai had finished both sword and scabbard, and, stepping up to the giant's great chair, pretended to hand them to him. But, as the giant was off his guard, he lifted the sword, and brought it down on Garnard's neck, so that he cut off his head. Before his followers could lay hands on Kai and Bedivere, the knights rushed out upon them, and slew them all. Then, having loaded themselves with gold and jewels, but above all with the precious sword, they set forth again for Arthur's palace.

This time they reached it in safety, and, having told their story, asked the advice of the King as to which of the six remaining quests they should first undertake. To seek out Mabon, the son of Modron, was Arthur's decision; and for this undertaking he chose Uriel because he could understand the speech of both animals and birds, as well as that of all strange men; and Idwel, because he was Mabon's kinsman, with Kai and Bedivere, because they were known never to turn back from any adventure until it was accomplished.

So these four set out upon their quest.

Now, Mabon had been lost so long ago that not the oldest man on the earth, nor their great-grandfathers before them, had ever heard anything at all about him. But Idwel remembered that many birds and beasts live much longer than the oldest man, so they determined to seek out the oldest of these.

"And who," said they, "could be older than the Ousel of Deepdell? Let us seek her help."

So they made their way through a great forest till they came to a shadowy place, where on a small stone sat the Ousel of Deepdell; and her they implored to tell them if she knew anything of Mabon, son of Modron, who was taken from between his mother and the wall when he was only three days old.

"When I first came here," answered the Ousel gravely, "I was but a fledgling. On this spot where I now sit stood a smith's stone anvil. Since then no hand has touched it, but every evening I have pecked at it with my beak as I smoothed my feathers before sleeping. Now all that remains of it is this little pebble upon which I sit. Yet through all the years that have passed while this change took place I have never heard of Mabon, the son of Modron. But do not despair: I will take you to a race of creatures who were made before me, and them ye shall inquire of again."

Then she took them to a place where, at the foot of an ancient oak, lay the Stag of the Fern Brake. Of him they once more asked the question: "Dost thou know anything of Mabon, son of Modron, parted from his mother when three days old?"

The Stag answered: "When first I came here this great forest was a vast plain, in which grew one little oak sapling. This sapling became in time an oak-tree, and after its long lifetime gradually decayed until it became this stump. Now, an oak-tree is three hundred years in growing, three hundred years in its full strength, and three hundred years in its decay. Yet in all this time I have never heard aught of Mabon, son of Modron. But, since ye are Arthur's knights, I will take you to one who was made before my time." Then he led them to the Owl of Darkdingle.

"When first I came here," said the Owl from his dark cavernous home when he heard their question, "this valley was covered with a vast wood. It decayed away, and another grew up, and after that had withered away, a third, which now ye see. But never have I heard of the man whom ye seek. Yet, since ye are Arthur's knights, I will take ye to the oldest creature in the world—to the Eagle of the Aldergrove."

So thither they went, and when he heard their question the Eagle answered: "When I first arrived, there was a rock in this place so high that I could perch on its top and peck at the stars, and so long have I been here that now it is but a few inches high. Never have I heard of this man save once, and that was when I visited the Lone Lake. There I stuck my claws into a salmon, hoping to kill him for my supper; but he dragged me into deep water, so that I barely escaped with my life. But when I went with all my band to slay him, he sent ambassadors, and made good peace with me, and came and begged me to take fifty fish-spears out of his back. He, if anyone can, will tell you what you want to know, and I will be your guide to him."

So they journeyed on till they reached a great blue lake, hidden in the depths of the forest, and there they found the Salmon of the Lone Lake. He heard their question, and looking at them very wisely, replied: "Such wrong as I have never found elsewhere have I found under the walls of Gloucester Castle, on the River Severn, up which I travel with every tide. And that ye may know it is so, come, two of ye, and travel thither upon my shoulders."

Then Kai and Uriel came down to the water, and stood upon the shoulders of the Salmon of Lane Lake, who swam with them down the Severn, and brought them under the walls of Gloucester Castle.

"Hark!" said the Salmon; and as they listened, a voice was heard from the dungeon wall wailing in deepest sorrow and woe. Then Uriel cried: "Whose voice is this that moans within this gloomy cell?"

"Alas!" wailed the voice, "'tis that of Mabon, the son of Modron, shut up eternally in the prison of Gwyn, son of Nith, King of Faerie. Here I, the Elfin Huntsman, ever young, am shut out eternally from the sight of wood and fell and the joyful chase which is my birthright."

"Canst thou be ransomed with silver and gold?" asked Uriel.

"No," answered Mabon; "if ever I am rescued from this cruel place it must be by battle and strife."

Then Uriel and Kai returned to their companions.

Seeing that this was the kind of adventure that Arthur loved, they journeyed back to the King, and told him all. So he prepared a great army, and marched by land to attack Gloucester Castle. But while he fought before the gates, Kai and Bedivere had sailed down the river on the shoulders of the Salmon of Lone Lake, and, finding the water-side portion of the Castle unprotected, they broke through the wall, and carried off Mabon, the son of Modron, and he returned with them to Arthur's Court.

V. How Prince Kilhugh won his Bride

While Arthur and his knights were discussing which of the Impossible Tasks should next be undertaken, it so happened that a certain prince, named Gwyther, who was also one of Arthur's knights, was walking over a mountain in his own country, the Land of the Dawn.

And as he walked, deep in thought, he heard a sad little cry. Up and down he looked, but nothing could he see that could explain such mournful cry. But presently it came again from under his very feet, and there he saw an ant-hill. Inside the ant-hill the little creatures were wailing piteously, for the heath on the mountain-side was afire, and in a short time their kingdom would be all in a blaze.

Then Prince Gwyther drew his sword, and cut off the ant-hill at a blow, and threw it into a place of safety.

"Our grateful thanks are thine," cried the ants. "Now tell us what we can do for thee in return, Prince Gwyther of the Land of the Dawn."

The Prince pondered a moment, and then replied: "All the world knows that Kilhugh, one of the Companions of Arthur, seeking the hand of the fair Olwen, is required by her father to bring him the nine bushels of flax seed sown in his field to make the wedding veil for his bride. If one grain is missing the marriage will be forbidden; and, though we are Arthur's knights, not one of us can find these tiny seeds. Now, can ye do this task for me?"

"That will we joyfully," cried the ants, and they made their way in haste to the field of Thornogre Thistlehair, Chief of the Giants.

When evening began to fall they returned to the Land of the Dawn, where Prince Gwyther had set up a bushel measure. Up its sides they climbed, each with a seed in its mouth; and nine times they filled the measure, until only one seed was wanting. "'Tis well," they cried; "the lame emmet has not yet come home." And before nightfall the lame emmet toiled up to the bushel measure, and dropped in the last seed.

So the nine bushels of flax seed were taken to the castle of Arthur, and given to Prince Kilhugh.

Then said King Arthur: "Let us now go to Ireland to seek for the Cauldron of Cruseward the Steward of Odgar, the Irish King."

Now, this cauldron, as you will remember, was of such a kind that when food for a coward was cooked in it the food remained as it was at first, but if for a brave man it was ready for eating directly it was placed in the pot. So it was very precious; and when Arthur's request for it was received by Odgar, Cruseward replied in wrath: "Not a glimpse of my cauldron shall he obtain, even if it would give him all the blessings in the world; much less will I give it him altogether."

Then Arthur called together his men of war, and sailed over the stormy seas to Ireland. When the people saw him in battle array, they were afraid, and counselled Odgar to receive him peaceably. So Odgar sent friendly messages, and invited him to a banquet in his palace.

Now when the banquet was over, Odgar was about to give presents to his guests, but Arthur would take nothing. He wanted naught, he said, but the Cauldron of Cruseward. When Cruseward heard this, he thundered out: "Nay, King Arthur, I will never give it to thee. If thou couldst have it for the asking it would have been given at the bidding of King Odgar, not at thine."

When Bedivere heard this rude reply he was very angry, and, rushing upon him, seized the cauldron, and set it on the shoulders of Arthur's Cauldron-

Bearer. Then swords were drawn, and the men of Arthur's host fell upon Cruseward and his followers, and slew them. Thus they carried off the cauldron, and bore it, full of Irish gold, back to the Island of the Mighty.

After this adventure they set forth to obtain the Charmed Balsam that was guarded by the Jet-Black Sorceress, daughter of the Snow-White Sorceress, at the Brook of Sorrow, on the edge of the Twilight Land. And when they approached the dismal cavern where she dwelt, King Arthur was joined by Gwyn of the Twilight Land, and Gwyther from the Land of the Dawn, who, knowing the Sorceress and her power, advised that two of his attendants should first be sent into the cave. Directly the first appeared the Sorceress seized him by the hair, and threw him down, and trampled on him. The second dragged her away from him, but could do nothing against her, for she kicked them and beat them and thrust them forth again.

Then Arthur would have gone in himself; but Prince Gywn and Prince Gwyther prevented him, saying it would not be a fitting adventure for so great a king, and persuaded him to send in the two Tall Brothers. But these two were so ill treated by the Sorceress that they came out more dead than alive, and had to be lifted on to their horses. Then, when he saw his followers so ill used, nothing could keep Arthur back. He rushed into the cave, and with one stroke of his dagger, killed the wicked Sorceress, while Kai carried off the Charmed Balsam.

They next set out to hunt the Boar-headed Branch-breaker; but soon they heard that no man could pluck out the tusk from the living head of this terrible animal but Odgar, King of Ireland.

With some difficulty they persuaded him to accompany them; but at length the huntsmen gathered together, with him at their head, and a great hunt for the boar began. The swiftest dogs could not bring the animal to bay, until at length Arthur's own hound, Cavall, brought him to the ground, and Odgar rushed up to pull out the tusk; but he would have been killed, had not Kai been there to strike the Branch-breaker down directly Odgar had plucked it out.

There yet remained to seek out the jewelled scissors and comb that were between the ears of Burstingboar, the Wide-Waster.

Now, this Burstingboar had laid waste a great part of Ireland, so that all men went in terror of him; and, that the heroes might not be misled about the curious things said to lie between his ears, Merlin was sent to Ireland to seek him out and see if it were as the giant had said.

So Merlin tracked Burstingboar to his den on Cold Blast Ridge, and, having changed himself into a bird, flew down into a thicket close by. From thence he could see the creature lying on the ground, with his seven young boars at his side, and between his ears twinkled the jewels of the scissors and the comb. Then Merlin thought it was a sad thing that the heroes should lose their lives for such things, and determined to try to carry them off himself. So he flew upon the head of Burstingboar, and tried to snatch up the razor; but all he really got was a great bristle. Then Burstingboar rose up in a great rage, foaming at the mouth. He could see no one; but a fleck of the poisonous foam fell upon Merlin, and hurt him so that he never quite recovered.

When he heard this news, Arthur gathered together such a number of brave knights and squires that the Irish feared he was about to attack their land, but when he told them he had come to deliver them from the dreaded Burstingboar, their joy knew no bounds. And so it was arranged that those Irish who had joined his host should first attack the boar; then, if he still lived, he should be attacked by Arthur's own knights; and if by that time he were not slain, Arthur should himself hunt him on the third day.

But the first day and the second saw the boar triumphant; and when Arthur took his turn he fought for nine days and nights without even wounding the creature or one of his cubs. At the end of that time all the knights besought Arthur to tell them the secret about the boar, which all this time he had kept.

Then Arthur told them that the creature had once been a king, but for his sins and his great pride had been changed into a boar. And he sent Uriel to confer with him concerning the jewelled comb and scissors. But when Uriel spoke gently to him, bidding him deliver these up at the request of Arthur, the boar grew very fierce, and said: "Not only shall Arthur never even see these jewels, but I with my young ones will go forthwith and harry the land of Arthur, doing all the hurt to it that we can."

When they heard this news all the host arose at dawn to prevent them leaving Ireland; but when they looked towards the sea, there was the boar with his young ones swimming far away to the coast of Britain. And before the King could cross the Irish Sea, the boars had landed at Milford Haven, and destroyed every living thing in the neighbourhood.

Then terror fell on all the land, and eagerly men looked for Arthur to come to their aid, who, when he arrived, set out at once with a crowd of mighty huntsmen to kill the beasts. But it was exceeding hard to find the boar, though his tracks were well marked by the ruin of flocks and men; and when they did come up with him, he slew with his mighty tusks a full half-dozen of Arthur's followers, and dashed off to a mountain-top, where they lost all sign of him: neither man nor dog could tell whither he had disappeared.

At last they heard that the boars were ravaging a valley some miles away. Thither they followed, and after a hard struggle they killed the young boars one by one. But after a long pursuit Burstingboar vanished again, so completely this time that the host returned to Cornwall, thinking he must have left the land.

Scarcely had Arthur entered his palace when a breathless messenger rushed into the hall.

"Arise!" he cried. "The boar is ruining thy domain, trampling down towers and towns, uprooting trees, and killing men and cattle on all sides, and he is now coming over the mountains to do the same in Cornwall."

Then Arthur made this speech to his followers:

"Men of the Island of the Mighty, Burstingboar, the Wide-Waster, has slain many of our bravest men, but he shall never enter Cornwall while I live. You may do as you please; but for me, I will no longer hunt him, but shall meet him face to face."

Forthwith he posted men at various spots to prevent the creature from landing, and then rode up to the river's brink. As he arrived, suddenly, with a great rush, Burstingboar sprang out of the forest, and tried to cross on his way to Cornwall. But Arthur and his companions drove their horses into the water, and followed him, and somehow or other seized him by his fore feet as he scrambled up the bank, and flung him back into the river; and as he fell, Mabon, the son of Modron, caught the razor from behind one of his ears, and Kenneder the Wild snatched the scissors from behind the other.

Yet, even while they did this, Burstingboar upreared himself from the water, dashed up the river-bank, and disappeared. Then all the host followed, but they only came up to him when he had got well into Cornwall. Then a desperate fight began. By harassing him all day they managed to keep him from ravaging the land, and when he tried to get into Devon they were too many for him. Over the moors, down the coombs, up the hills, they chased him, till at length, being desperate, he turned, and made for the sea. In he plunged, but, though the pursuing horses stayed their feet at the water's edge, those two good hounds, Raceapace and Boundoft, who had followed him so long, could not hold themselves back, but plunged in after him into the waves. For long the heroes watched his course, with those two fierce dogs close behind him; but from that day to this nothing more has ever been heard of either Burstingboar or the two hounds.

Now, all the Impossible Tasks had been fulfilled, and joyfully did Prince Kilhugh ride to the giant's castle to claim his bride. But Thornogre Thistlehair looked on in gloomy silence as the marvels were spread out before him; he allowed himself to be shaven and combed; but though he could not refuse to give the Prince his daughter's hand, he openly said that he did it with no good will. Then the herdsman's son stood forth, and cried: "O giant, three and twenty of my brothers thou hast foully slain, and defrauded my father of his heritage. For these things thou shalt surely die by my hand to-day."

So he dragged him by his hair to the castle battlements, and, being very strong, he slew him there, and cut off his head. And the castle was given to the herdsman; but Kilhugh married fair Olwen, and they were happy ever after as long as they both lived.

From the "Mabinogion," A Welsh Romance. Thirteenth century A.D.

THE LADY OF THE FOUNTAIN

I. The Tale of Kynon

Kynon was the only son of his father and mother, and a very brave and daring young knight. He thought there was nothing in the world too mighty for him to do; and after he had achieved all the possible adventures in his own country, he equipped himself with horse and armour, and went forth to journey in desert and unknown lands.

One day it chanced that he came to the fairest valley in the world, where all the trees grew to the same height; a river ran through the valley, and a path was by the side of the river. He followed this path till midday, and travelled along the remainder of the valley till evening, and at length came to a large and shining castle, at the foot of which was a rushing torrent. Before the gates stood two youths with yellow, curling locks, wearing golden frontlets upon their heads and garments of yellow satin, with gold clasps on their insteps. Each of them held in his hand an ivory bow, and their arrows were winged with peacock's feathers. Their daggers had blades of gold and hilts of whalebone, and they played with them as they stood, shooting them to and fro. They allowed Kynon to pass into the courtyard, and there he saw a man, in the prime of life, also clad in a robe of yellow satin, and round the top of his yellow mantle was a band of gold lace. He received Kynon with great courtesy, and at once conducted him into the hall of the castle. In the hall sat four and twenty damsels embroidering satin at a window, and they were all so very fair that the eyes of Kynon were almost dazzled at the sight of so much beauty. They rose at his coming, and six of them took his horse, and unbuckled his armour; six more took his weapons, and washed them in a basin till they shone like the sun; another six spread cloths on the table and prepared meat; and the last six took off his soiled cloak and doublet, and put on garments of fine linen and yellow satin, with a broad gold band round the mantle. Then they gave him cushions of red linen on which to sit, and brought bowls of silver full of water wherein to wash, and towels, some of green linen, some of white. Presently, when all was ready, they sat down to eat at a silver table, with cloths of the finest linen, and the meats that were brought were of the most delicious flavour in the world.

At length, when the stranger's hunger was appeased, the Man in Yellow began to inquire who he was, and what was the cause of his journey.

And Kynon told him that he was trying to find out if anyone were his superior, or whether he could gain the mastery over all. The Man in Yellow smiled, saying: "If I did not fear that harm would come to thee I would show thee that thou seekest."

Then Kynon implored him to make trial of him, and at length the man agreed. "Sleep here to-night," said he, "and on the morning arise early, and take the road upward through the valley till you come to the wood by which you came. A little way within the wood you will find a path branching off to the right. Follow this until you come to a large, sheltered glade, with a mound in the centre. On the top of the mound you will see a black man of great size, larger than two men of this world. He has but one foot, and one eye in the middle of his forehead. In his hand he holds a club which no two men could lift. He is exceedingly ill-favoured to look at, and he is the warden of that wood. And round about him you will see grazing a thousand wild animals. Inquire of him the way out of the glade, and he will point out the road which will lead you to that of which you are in quest."

Next morning Kynon arose very early, and rode away. All came to pass as the Man in Yellow had said, except that the black man was of huger size and his club looked far heavier than Kynon had been led to suppose. When Kynon saw the thousand animals browsing around the mound and the black man sitting on the top of it, he asked what power he held over those creatures.

"I will show thee, little man," said he; and, taking up his club, he struck one of the stags a great blow. The stag brayed loudly, and at the sound all the animals came together, as many as the stars in the sky, so that Kynon scarcely found room to stand. Serpents were there, and dragons, and every kind of beast. Then the black man looked at them, and bade them go feed; and they all bowed their heads, and did homage to him ere they departed.

Then Kynon asked the way out of the glade; and when the man knew his reason he said to him: "Take the path that leads towards the head of the glade, and ascend the woody steeps until you reach the summit; there you will find an open space like a large valley, and in the midst of it a tall tree, with branches greener than the greenest pine-trees.

"Beneath this tree is a fountain, and by the fountain a marble slab, and on the slab a silver bowl attached by a silver chain. Take the bowl, and throw a bowlful of water on the slab, and you shall see what will happen. And if you do not find trouble in that adventure you need not seek it during the rest of your life."

So Kynon did as he had said, and found the fountain, and threw a bowlful of water upon the slab. And immediately there came a mighty peal of thunder, so that the earth shook. With the thunder came a shower of hailstones, so heavy that each one pierced to the bone, and Kynon could only endure it by placing his shield over his own and his horse's head. After that the weather became fair; but when he looked at the tree, behold! there was not a single leaf left upon it. Then a flock of birds came, and alighted on the tree, and never was heard such sweet strains as those they sang; and while he was listening to the birds a murmuring voice rose through the valley, like a gust of wind, which said:

"O knight, what has brought you hither? What evil have I done to you that you should act towards me and my possessions as you have this day? Do you not know that the shower to-day has left alive neither beast nor man that was exposed to it?"

Scarcely had the voice died away when there appeared a knight clad in black velvet, riding a coal-black horse, who made a rush at Kynon then and there. And the onset was so furious, and Kynon so little prepared, that he was overthrown. Then the Black Knight passed the shaft of his lance through the bridle-rein of Kynon's horse, and, without a glance at his fallen adversary, rode off the way he had come. There was nothing left for the fallen knight but to make his way back to the castle. The black man jeered aloud at him as he passed through the glade, and, with much anger and mortification, the knight hurried on to the castle of the Man in Yellow. There he was received with the utmost hospitality; and no one alluded to his adventure, nor did he mention it to any. On the next day he found, ready saddled, a dark bay horse, with nostrils as red as scarlet, and, mounted on this, he returned to Arthur's Court.

II. The Tale of Owain

When Kynon had related at Arthur's Court the story of his adventure with the Black Knight, one of his companions, Owain by name, said: "Is it not befitting that one of us go and discover this place?"

"It is very well to talk about it," said Sir Kai, "but 'tis harder to carry it out."

Then Owain went away, and prepared his horse and his armour, and very early next morning he rode away in the direction which Kynon had pointed out to him.

In due time he reached the castle, and was kindly received by the Man in Yellow, and set down before a very excellent meal. And the four and twenty maidens seemed even lovelier to Owain than they had to Kynon.

When they asked him his errand Owain replied that he was in quest of the knight who guards the fountain; and the Yellow Man, though very reluctantly, pointed out the way. All happened to Owain as it had to Kynon, save that the shower seemed more violent and the song of the birds even sweeter than before. And as they sang the Black Knight appeared, and rode violently upon Owain; but he was prepared to receive him, and they fought fiercely together. Their lances broke with the shock of their attack, and, drawing their swords, they fought until Owain struck the knight a blow which pierced through helmet, skull, and brain.

Then the Black Knight, knowing he had received a mortal blow, turned his horse, and fled. But Owain pursued hard after him until they came to a lordly castle. When they reached the gate the Black Knight was allowed to enter; but Owain was so close behind that, when the portcullis fell, it struck his horse behind the saddle, and cut him in two, carrying away the rowels of the spurs which were on Owain's heels. So the rowels and part of the horse were outside and Owain was shut up inside with the other part of the horse between the two gates, for the inner one was closed. As the knight stood wondering what would happen next he saw through an opening in the upper part of the gate a street facing him, with a row of houses on either side; and from one of these houses came out a maiden, with yellow, curling locks, dressed in yellow satin, with shoes of parti-coloured leather. She approached the gate, and desired him to open it. "Truly, lady," said Owain ruefully, "I can no more open it for you than you can for me."

"That is very sad," said the damsel; "yet it is the part of every woman to do what she can to succour you, for you are a loyal squire of dames, so I will do whatever is in my power for you. Take this ring, and put it on your finger, with the stone inside your hand, and close your hand upon the stone. As long as you conceal it, it will conceal you. Presently, when they have consulted together, they will come to fetch you, in order to put you to death, and will be much upset when they cannot find you. But I shall sit on the horse-block yonder, and you will see me though I cannot see you. Come, therefore, and put your hand upon my shoulder, that I may know you are near; and whichever way I go, do you follow me."

So Owain vanished from the sight of men, and sorely grieved were his foes when they came to seek him and found only part of his horse. But he found the maiden, and laid his hand upon her shoulder; and she led him to a splendid chamber, where even the nails were painted in beautiful colours, and there she gave him abundance of food in silver dishes, and left him to rest. Now, on that night the nobleman who owned the castle, whom Owain had so grievously wounded, died; and the maiden of the golden locks presently brought Owain to a window from whence he might see the funeral procession. And foremost among the mourners walked the Countess of that domain. She was so very beautiful that Owain fell deeply in love with her, and said to the maiden: "Verily, there goes the woman I love best in the world."

"Truly," said the maiden, "she too shall love you not a little, and I will go woo for thee."

So the maiden, whose name was Luned, went to the chamber of her mistress the Countess, and found her weeping, because now the Black Knight was slain, there was no one to defend her dominions. For so it was that, so long as the fountain was safe, all was well, but if that were not defended, all her lands would soon be lost.

Then Luned said: "Surely you know that no one can defend the fountain except he be a knight of Arthur's household. Let me go to Arthur's Court, and I will bring back with me a warrior who can guard the fountain as well as, or even better than, he who kept it formerly."

"That will be a hard task," said the Countess. "Go, however, and make good that which thou hast promised."

But Luned did not go to Arthur's Court; she went instead to the chamber of Owain, and, having warned him to wait until it was due time, hid herself as long as it would have taken to travel to the Court.

Then she brought Owain a coat and mantle of yellow satin, on which were bands of broad gold lace; and for his feet shoes of softest leather, fastened by golden clasps in the shape of lions; and thus they proceeded to the chamber of the Countess.

But when they arrived the Countess looked steadfastly upon Owain, and said: "Luned, this knight has not the appearance of a traveller."

"Well, lady, he is none the worse for that," said Luned.

"I am certain," said the Countess, "that this is the man who killed my master, the Black Knight."

"So much the better for you, lady," replied Luned, "for if he had not been stronger than your master, he could not have killed him. There is no use in crying over spilt milk."

Then the Countess looked again on Owain, and when she saw he was a very goodly knight, and courageous withal, she began to return his affection for her; and soon afterwards they were married. So Owain defended the fountain with lance and sword; and whenever a knight came there, he overthrew him, and ransomed him for his full worth, and what he then obtained he divided among his barons and his knights, so that he became very much beloved. And so three years passed away.

III. The further Adventures of Owain

When three long years had gone by, King Arthur began to get very sad because he heard nothing of his good knight Owain. And when the others saw his sadness they suggested that he and the men of his household should go and seek Owain. So they set off; and Kynon was their guide. They spent the night at the castle of the Man in Yellow, and he and his twenty-four damsels waited upon them with the utmost hospitality. In the morning they set off for the wood, and, passing the black man, they came to the fountain. Then Sir Kai begged that he might throw the water on the slab and receive the adventure that first befell. All happened as before, save that several of the attendants were killed by the hail-storm; and as they stood listening to the song of the birds, a knight clad in black satin, riding on a coal-black horse, spurred up to Sir Kai, and in a few minutes Sir Kai was overthrown.

Then the knight rode off, and the host of Arthur encamped as darkness drew on.

The next day Sir Kai met the Black Knight again, and this time was wounded very sorely. Then each of the knights in turn fought, and all were overthrown save one, and he was called Gwalchmai. The fight between him and the Black Knight was very fierce, but at length a heavy blow broke the helmet of Gwalchmai, and showed his face. And, behold, the Black Knight threw down his sword, and embraced him, saying: "Little did I know that you were my cousin Gwalchmai." Then did Gwalchmai know the voice of Owain, and embraced him, and brought him to Arthur, and everyone was glad to see the long-lost knight again.

So all the company proceeded to the castle of the Countess of the Fountain, and there partook of a great banquet, which had been three years preparing; for Owain had always said that Arthur would come to seek him. And when all was over Arthur prepared to depart, but first he sent a message to the Countess, begging her to permit Owain to go and visit him for the space of three months. So Owain departed, though much against the will of his Countess; and when he was once more among his kindred and friends he forgot all about his wife and the People in Yellow, and stayed away three years instead of three months. At the end of these three years, as Owain sat one day at meat in the royal city of Caerleon-on-Usk, there rode through the doorway of the hall a damsel on a bay horse covered with foam, wearing a bridle and saddle of gold; and the damsel was clad in a robe of yellow satin. She came up to Owain, and, taking the ring from off his hand, "Thus," she said, "shall be treated the deceiver, the traitor, the faithless and the disgraced."

Then she turned her horse's head, and rode away.

Then was Owain deeply ashamed and sorrowful; and on the next day he left the Court, and wandered to the distant parts of the country and to waste places and barren mountains. And he stayed there until his clothes were worn out and his body wasted away and his hair grown long. His only companions were the wild beasts with whom he fed, and they grew to love him as their friend; but after a time he became so weak that he could no longer abide with them, so he descended from the mountains into the fairest park in all the world, which was said to belong to a widowed countess.

One day the Countess and her maidens were walking by a lake that was in the middle of the park, when they saw in the pathway the prostrate figure of a man. At first they thought he was dead; but they went near, and touched him, and found there was life in him, though he was very much exhausted. So the Countess returned to the castle, and sent one of her maidens with a flask full of precious balsam to the sick man, together with a horse and a good suit of clothes, and said:

"Go with these, and place them near the man we saw just now. Anoint him with the balsam near his heart, and if there is still life in him he will arise through the strength of the balsam. Then watch what he will do."

The maiden departed, and forthwith poured the whole of the balsam on Owain, and left the horse and the garments close by, and hid herself, and watched what would happen. Presently he began to move his hands, then his arms, and then all at once he rose up, and was ashamed to see how ragged and dirty he looked. Then he perceived the horse, and the garments; so he washed in the lake, and crept to the horse, and with difficulty clothed himself, and clambered on to the saddle. Then came the maiden from her hiding-place, and he was rejoiced to see her, and asked her to whom the park belonged.

"Truly," said she, "a widowed countess owns park and castle, which are all that are left to her of two noble earldoms left to her by her late husband. All the rest has been taken from her by a neighbouring earl because she refused to become his wife."

"That is a pity," said Owain. And the maiden conducted him to the castle, and brought him to a pleasant room, and left him there. Then she went to the Countess, and gave her back the flask. "Ha! damsel," said her mistress, "where is all the balsam?" "Have I not used it all?" said she. "O maiden," said the Countess, "thou hast wasted for me seven-score pounds' worth of ointment on an unknown stranger. However, now that he is here, wait thou upon him until he is quite recovered."

So the maiden tended Owain, and gave him meat and drink and medicine until he was well again. And in three months he was as comely a knight as ever he had been before. One day he heard a great tumult in the castle, and asked the maiden the cause thereof. She told him that the earl whom she had mentioned before had come against the Countess with a large army to force her to marry him. "Has she a horse and arms to spare?" asked Owain. "She has the best in the world," said she.

"Then go and beg the loan of them," said Owain, "that I may go and have a look at this earl." "I will," said the maiden. So she made her request to the Countess; but the lady laughed a bitter laugh, and said: "He may as well have them to-day as my enemy to-morrow; but I know not what he would do with them."

Then they brought out a beautiful black horse, with a beechen saddle, and a suit of armour for man and horse; and Owain armed himself, and rode forth, attended by two pages. When they came in sight of the enemy they could not see where the army ended, it was so great; but Owain asked where the earl himself was, and when he was pointed out, he sent the pages back to the castle, and rode forward till he met the earl. And Owain was now so strong that he drew the earl completely out of the saddle, and turned his horse's head towards the castle, and, although it was no easy task, brought the earl to the gate. When they had entered, he gave the earl as a gift to the Countess, and said to her: "Lo, here is a return to you for your wondrous balsam."

Then the earl restored to the Countess her two earldoms in ransom for his life, and for his freedom he gave her half his own domains and all his jewels and gold and silver.

After this Owain departed from the castle, though all honoured him greatly and begged him to stay with them. But he was still ashamed and sorrowful at heart, and preferred rather to ride forth into desert places again.

One day, as he was journeying through a wood, he heard a great uproar, and, riding forward, found a great craggy mound, on the side of which was a grey rock. In the rock was a cleft, and in the cleft a serpent; and near by stood a black lion, and every time the lion moved to go hence the serpent darted towards him to attack him.

Then Owain unsheathed his sword, and struck the serpent, and cut him in two, and went on his way. But, strange to say, the lion followed him, and played about him like a dog. All that day they travelled together; and at night Owain dismounted, and turned his horse loose in a woody meadow. And he kindled a fire, the lion bringing him wood enough to last for three nights. Then the lion disappeared, and after a while returned bearing a fine, large roebuck, which he laid before Owain; and when it was skinned and roasted, it made an excellent supper for them both. As he was eating, he heard a deep sigh near him, which was repeated three times.

"Who is there?" asked Owain. "A mortal maiden," was the reply. "Who art thou?" he asked again. And the voice replied: "I am Luned, the handmaiden of the Countess of the Fountain. In this stone vault am I imprisoned on account of the knight who came from Arthur's Court and married my Countess. For a short time only he stayed with her, and then went away, and has never returned—and he was the friend I loved most in the world. And one day two of the pages of the Countess's chamber reviled him, and called him ill names, and I told them that they two were not a match for him alone. Then they imprisoned me in this stone cell, and said I should be put to death unless he came himself to deliver me by a certain day—and that is the day after to-morrow. But I have no one to send to seek him for me. And his name is Owain, the son of Urien."

Then Owain said: "Art thou certain that if the knight knew all this, he would come to your rescue?"

"I am most certain of it," said she.

So Owain bade her hope for the best, and meantime bade her tell him if there were any place near, where he could get lodging for the night. She bade him follow the river, so he rode along till he came to a very fine castle. The Earl who ruled over the place received him very hospitably, and good fodder was given to his horse. But the lion went and lay down in the horse's manger, so that none of the men of the castle dared to approach him. Meantime Owain had been brought in to supper; and very soon the lion came, and sat between his knees, and shared his food. Then Owain noticed that everyone in the castle was very sorrowful. The Earl sat on one side of him, and his fair young daughter on the other; and he never saw anyone look as sad as they.

In the middle of supper the Earl began to bid Owain welcome, adding: "Heaven knows it is not thy coming which makes us sorrowful, but we have good cause for care."

"How is that?" asked Owain.

"I have two sons," replied the Earl, "who went yesterday to hunt upon the mountains. But on the mountains lives an evil monster who kills men and devours them, and he has seized my sons; and to-morrow he will bring them here, and will devour them before my eyes, unless I will deliver my sweet daughter into his hands. He has the form of a man, but the strength of a giant, and no one can do aught against him."

"Truly this is a hard case," said Owain. "And what wilt thou do?"

"Heaven knows," said the Earl. "But I can never give up my young daughter to be destroyed by him; yet I cannot bear to lose my two brave sons."

So no more was said, and Owain stayed there that night.

Next morning a great noise was heard as the giant entered the courtyard, dragging behind him the two youths by the hair of their heads. Then Owain put on his armour, and went out to fight the giant, and the lion followed him. The giant made a great rush upon the knight; and the lion fought on Owain's side, more fiercely than his master. At length the giant said: "I could easily settle this business with you were it not for the animal that is with you." So Owain shut the lion up inside the castle walls, and went back to fight the giant as before. But the lion heard that it was going ill with Owain; and he roared very loud, and climbed up till he reached the top of the castle, and then sprang down from the walls, and joined his master. And very soon he gave the giant such a stroke with his paw that the monster fell down dead.

Then the Earl was full of gratitude, and begged Owain to remain with him; but he would only stay one more night, and on the morrow set out for the meadow where Luned was imprisoned in the mound. When he reached the spot, he found a great fire kindled, and two youths with curling auburn hair were leading the maiden forth to cast her in the fire.

"Why are you treating her thus?" asked Owain.

They told him of the compact that was between them concerning the maiden. "Owain has failed her," said they, "therefore she must be burnt according to our agreement."

"Well," said Owain, "I know him for a good knight, and if he had known of the maiden's peril he would have come to her rescue; but if you will accept me in his stead I will do battle for her."

This was agreed; and the fight began. But the two were together stronger than Owain, and he was hard beset. Then the lion came to his help, and they two were stronger than the young men. So they said to him: "Chieftain, we did not agree to fight with thy lion, but only with thee." Then Owain shut the lion up in the stone vault where the maiden had been imprisoned, and blocked up the entrance with stones, and returned to the fight. But he was weak from loss of blood, and the young men pressed hard upon him; and the lion roared like thunder when he heard that his master was in trouble, and he burst through the wall, and rushed upon the young men, and slew them both.

So Luned was saved, and glad was she when she found it was Owain indeed who had come to her rescue. Together they sought the dominions of the Countess of the Fountain; and she and Owain and the lion and Luned lived all happily together for the rest of their lives.

From the "Mabinogion."

THE STORY OF KING LUD

King Lud was King of Britain, and a very mighty warrior. He built for himself a fine castle, and lived in it most part of the year. It was called Caer Lud, and afterwards Caer London, but after the stranger race came to Britain it was just called London. Lud had a brother, Llevelys, whom he loved very dearly; and he married a princess of France, and became king of that land, and ruled it well and happily. Now, after some years three dismal plagues fell upon the island of Britain, such as no other land had ever known. The first was the plague of the Coranians. These Coranians were a certain people who knew every word that was said upon the island, however low it might be spoken, if only the wind met it. And because of this they could not be injured, for they knew all their enemies' plans beforehand.

The second plague was a terrible shriek that came on every May-eve over each hearth in the island of Britain. And the shriek pierced through the hearts of all, so that men lost their valour and strength, and women and children and young men and maidens their senses, and all the animals and trees and earth and waters were left barren.

The third plague was that whatever store of food and provisions might be laid up in the King's court, even if so much as a whole year's supply of meat and drink, none of it could ever be found except what was consumed in the first night.

Then King Lud was very sad at heart, because he knew not how to free his land from the dismal plagues. He called together all the nobles of his kingdom, and asked counsel as to what he should do in the midst of these afflictions. And they all advised him to go to France and seek the advice of Llevelys his brother, king of that land. So they made ready a fleet in secrecy and silence, lest the Coranian race should learn the cause of their journey; and Lud, with some of his chosen followers, set his face towards France. When Llevelys saw his brother's ship approaching, he went out to meet him, and embraced him with much joy. Then King Lud told him the purpose of his errand; and King Llevelys thought a while, and, being very wise, soon discovered the cause of those dismal plagues. But they dared not talk freely about them to each other, lest the wind should catch their words, and the Coranians have knowledge of their discourse. So Llevelys caused a long horn to be made of brass, and through this horn they discoursed. But whatever words they spoke into the horn one to the other neither of them could hear anything but harsh and unfriendly words.

Then Llevelys saw that there was a demon in the horn thwarting all their purposes, and caused wine to be put in to wash it out; and through the virtue of the wine the demon was driven away.

When this was done, Llevelys told his brother through the horn that he would give him some insects, which he must take and bruise in water. And when he returned to his kingdom he must call together all the people, both of his own race and the Coranians, as though with the idea of making peace between them. And when they were all together he must take the charmed water made with the bruised insects, and cast it over all alike. And the water would poison the race of the Coranians, but it would not harm those of his own people.

"The second plague," he said—"that of the weird shriek—is caused by a dragon. Another dragon of a foreign race is fighting with it, and striving to overcome it, and for this reason does your dragon make a fearful outcry once every year. This must you do to rid yourself of this plague: cause the island to be measured in its length and breadth, and in the place where you find the exact central point, cause a pit to be dug; and in the pit you must place a cauldron full of the best mead that can be made, with a covering of satin over the face of the cauldron. Then remain there watching, and presently you will see the dragons fighting a terrific fight. Presently they will take the form of dragons of the air; and lastly, when they are worn out with the fury of their fighting, they will fall upon the covering of the cauldron in the form of two pigs, and they will sink in, and the covering with them, till they reach the bottom of the cauldron; and they will drink up all the mead, and after that they will go to sleep. Then you must immediately fold the covering around them, and shut them up in the strongest vessel in your dominions, and hide them deep in the earth. And so long as they shall bide in that strong vessel no plague shall come from elsewhere upon the island of Britain.

"The third plague," continued Llevelys, "is caused by a mighty magician, who takes your meat and drink and stores of provisions. Through his illusions and charms he causes everyone to sleep. Therefore must you watch your food yourself. And, lest he should overcome you with sleep, have a cauldron of ice-cold water by your side, and if you begin to get drowsy, plunge into the cauldron."

Then Lud thanked his brother for his good counsel, and returned to his own land. And first he summoned a meeting of all the people, both of his own race and that of the Coranians; and he bruised the insects in water, and cast it over the heads of all of them. Immediately it destroyed all the race of the Coranians, but his own people were hurt not at all.

And this was the end of the first dismal plague.

Then he caused the land to be measured in its length and its breadth; and he found the central point in Oxford, and in that place he caused the pit to be dug and the cauldron of mead to be placed, with a covering of satin over the face of it. There he presently beheld the dragons fighting; and when they were weary, they fell into the mead under the shape of pigs, and when they had drunk up all the mead, they slept. And Lud folded the covering round them, and hid them in the strongest place he had on Snowdon. And so the fierce shriek ceased to be heard in his dominions; and this was the end of the second dismal plague.

When this was all ended, King Lud caused a very great banquet to be prepared in the Court. And when it was ready, he placed a cauldron of ice-cold water by his side, and sat down to watch over the banquet. And about the third watch of the night he heard sweet music and gentle songs, which lulled him to sleep. But when he found himself getting very drowsy, he went often into the ice-cold water. At length a man of great size, clad in strong, heavy armour, came in, bearing a hamper; and into this hamper he began to put all the food and provisions of meat and drink, and proceeded to go forth with it. And King Lud was so stupefied with astonishment that one hamper could possibly hold so much, that he had almost let him go. At last, however, he recovered his senses, and rushed after him, and cried: "Stay, stay. Though thou hast done me many insults and stolen much spoil ere now, yet shalt thou do so no more, unless thy skill in arms be better than mine." The magician instantly put down the hamper, and rushed upon him; and they fought so desperately that fire flew from their arms. At length the victory was to Lud, and he threw

the plague to the earth. Then the magician besought him for his life, and promised to serve him as his vassal, and put all his power in the hands of the King, if he would release him; and to this King Lud agreed.

And this was the end of the third dismal plague. From that time forth King Lud reigned in peace and happiness in the island of Britain.

From the "Mabinogion."

THE TALE OF TALIESIN

Tegid Voel and Caridwen his wife lived on an island in the midst of Lake Tegid. (Nowadays the lake is called Bala, and there is no island to be seen.) They had an elder son, a fair and comely youth, and a very beautiful daughter; but their youngest son was uglier than anyone in the whole world. This troubled his mother Caridwen at first; but she said to herself: "If he cannot be handsome, he shall, at anyrate, be very learned." Now, Caridwen was a witch, so she set to work to boil a Cauldron of Knowledge, of which the boiling must not cease for a year and a day. At the end of that time it would yield three drops of precious liquid, which would make whoever drank it wise for the rest of his life. She set Gwion Bach, who was passing by, to stir the cauldron, and a blind man named Morda to keep up the fire underneath; but, fearing that Gwion Bach had seen what she put into the cauldron, and would tell her secrets to others, she made up her mind to kill him directly he had done his work for her.

Now, one day, as the end of the year drew nigh, while Caridwen was in the fields gathering herbs, it chanced that the three magic drops flew out of the cauldron, and fell on the finger of Gwion Bach. They scalded his hand so that he promptly put it to his mouth, and sucked his fingers; and immediately he became very wise, and knew all that Caridwen meant to do to him, and his need of guarding against her wily plots! He fled from the house, therefore, and ran towards his own land; and the cauldron, left unstirred, burst in two, and the poisonous liquid ran out of the door, and into a stream where the horses of Gwyddno were drinking; and when they had drunk of the poisoned water they all died.

When Caridwen returned, and saw the year's work was lost, she took up a billet of wood, and began to beat the blind man Morda. But he answered: "You do wrong to beat me; the loss was not because of me."

"You speak truly," said Caridwen. "It was Gwion Bach who robbed me." And she set to running after him as fast as she could. He soon looked back, and saw her, and changed himself into a hare; for the magic liquid had given him many different kinds of skill. But as he fled, she changed herself into a grey-hound, and had nearly caught him up when he ran towards a river and changed himself into a fish. Then she became an otter, and chased him till in his weariness he took the form of a bird. But she at once changed herself into a hawk, and gave him no rest in the sky.

Just as he was in fear of death, he saw a heap of grains of wheat on the floor of a barn; so he dropped among them, and became one of the grains. Then Caridwen changed herself into a high-crested black hen, and scratched among the grains till she found him. She was just about to swallow him, when, with his last remaining effort of skill, he became a very beautiful little child, and when she looked at him she had not the heart to kill him on the spot. So she took her own form again, and, having put the child into a leathern bag, she cast him into the sea just below the weir of Gwyddno, which is not far from Aberystwith, on the 29th of April. Then Caridwen returned home again, and thought no more of the matter.

Now, it had been the custom on every May-day eve to go fishing in that weir, and every year fish were taken to the value of a hundred pounds. Its owner, Gwyddno, had an only son named Elphin, the most unlucky of youths, who was always needing and never getting. This year his father, pitying his ill fortune, granted to him all the weir should contain on May-day, in order to give him something wherewith to begin the world. So the nets were set to catch the fish below the weir, and next day Elphin hurried to see how many they had caught. But the nets were quite empty, and nothing was to be found but a leathern bag which had caught in one of the poles of the weir. Then said one of his companions: "Men were unfortunate before, but never so much as now, when your luck has turned away the fish from a weir that has been worth a hundred pounds every May-eve till now, when there is nothing but a skin in it."

"Perhaps," said Elphin, "the bag may have something in it which is worth a hundred pounds." So his friend hooked up the bag, and opened it, and there peeped out the bright face of a little lad. "See, what a bright face within the bag!" cried his companion. And Elphin said: "Let him be called Taliesin, then" (which means "bright or shining face"), and lifted the child gently on to his horse, and made it walk softly, and went homeward with a very heavy heart.

But as he rode along, the boy behind him sang to him a song of consolation so sweetly that Elphin was much amazed, and asked how he had learnt so beautiful a song. The child replied that, though he was very little, he was notwithstanding very wise.

Then Elphin asked if he were a mortal child or a spirit; upon which the boy sang another song, telling what he had been, and how he had fled from Caridwen, and how he came to be entangled in the weir.

When Elphin reached the house of his father, the latter asked him if his haul were good.

"Father," he answered, "I have caught a poet-minstrel."

"Alas! what good will that do thee?" said Gwyddno.

And Taliesin answered for himself: "He will do him more good than the weir ever did for thee."

Then Gwyddno looked at him, and said: "Art thou able to speak when thou art so little?" And the child replied: "I am better able to speak than thou to question." "What canst thou say?" asked Gwyddno. Upon which Taliesin sang a song of such wondrous beauty, that everyone hastened to the spot to hear the marvellous child.

Soon afterwards Elphin, with his usual ill luck, managed to offend the powerful King Maelgwn, who cast him into a dungeon barred by thirteen locked doors. But when father Gwyddno was lamenting his son's ill fate, the child Taliesin bade him be of good cheer, since he was going to rescue him. Setting off at daybreak he reached the King's palace at the time of the evening meal, and entered the hall just as the bards were beginning to sing the praises of the King, as was their custom every evening. Then Taliesin cast a spell upon these bards, so that instead of singing they could only pout out their lips and make mouths at the King. He forced them also, by his magic power, to tap their fingers on their mouths, as they tried in vain to sing, making a curious sound like "Bler-m! Bler-m!"

The King, naturally, thought they were treating him with great disrespect, and ordered one of his squires to give a blow to the chief bard; and the squire took a broom, and struck him on the head, so that he fell back on his seat. This rough treatment seemed to bring him to his senses, and he then explained that they could not help themselves, but had been put under a spell by a spirit, who was sitting in a corner of the hall under the form of a child. So the King ordered the squire to fetch the child; and Taliesin, nothing loth, was brought up to the head of the table. Being asked who he was and whence he came, he at once proceeded to sing another wonderful song, in which he informed them that he was the chief bard of Elphin, that his native country was the land of

Cherubim, but that at present he was dwelling upon this earth, and might even stay here until the Judgment Day.

The King and his nobles marvelled greatly, for they had never heard the like from a boy so young as he. But as he was the bard of Elphin, who had offended His Majesty, the King determined that his own bards should get the better of him in song. So he ordered the chief bard to stand forth, and then all the four and twenty of them, to strive with Taliesin. But when they came forward to do his bidding they could do no other than play "Bler-m! Bler-m!" on their lips.

Then the King, angry and disappointed, asked the boy Taliesin his errand.

And the child replied in song: "I am come to deliver Elphin, who is imprisoned in this castle, behind thirteen locks."

"I will never let him go," said the King.

Then Taliesin foretold that there should come up from the sea-marshes a wonderful golden worm, which would take revenge upon the King for his cruelty; but, finding his threat had no effect, he turned, and left the hall. Outside the castle he sang a charm to the wind, bidding it blow open the prison of Elphin; and while he thus sang, near the door, there suddenly uprose such a storm of wind that the King and his nobles crouched in terror, expecting that the castle would fall upon their heads. Directly he realised that this was the work of the mysterious child-bard he sent for Elphin from the prison, and implored Taliesin to stay the wind-storm, which he accordingly did. So Elphin was brought into the hall, loaded with chains; at sight of which Taliesin sang another charm song, and the chains immediately fell off his hands and feet. By this time the King was so full of admiration for the skill and wisdom of the boy that he begged him to take the spell off his own bards, and to test them with questions.

So Taliesin set them free from his charm, and then began to rain questions upon them.

"Why is a stone hard?"

"Why is a thorn sharp-pointed?"

"What is as salt as brine?"

"Who rides the gale?"

"Why is a wheel round?"

"Why is the speech of the tongue different from any other gift?"

These were some of the questions he put, and ended with: "If you and your bards are able, let them give an answer to me, Taliesin."

But none of them could answer a single word.

Then the King dismissed them all with scorn; but still he would not let Elphin go free away.

Then Taliesin bade Elphin wager the King that he had a horse both better and swifter than the King's horses. The King accepted the challenge, and fixed day and time and place for the wager to be tried, and promised him his freedom if he should win the race. The King went thither with all his people and four and twenty of the swiftest horses he possessed. The course was marked out and the horses placed for running. Then came Taliesin with four and twenty twigs of holly, which he had burnt black, and he bade the youth who was to ride his master's horse to place them in his belt. Then he ordered him to let all the King's horses get before him, and, as he should overtake one horse after another, to strike the horse with a holly twig over the crupper, and then let that twig fall, and then to take another twig, and do the same to every one of the horses as he should overtake them.

Moreover, he bade the horseman to watch carefully where his own horse should stumble, and to throw down his cap on the spot. All this was done, and, behold! each horse that was struck with the holly twig began to lag behind, and the horse of Elphin easily won the race. When all was over, Taliesin brought his master to the spot where his horse had stumbled, and ordered workmen to dig a hole there; and when they had dug deep enough they found a cauldron full of gold. Then said Taliesin: "Elphin, take thou this as a reward for having taken me out of the weir and reared me from that time until now."

So Elphin went home a rich man to his father, and the work of Taliesin was accomplished.

From the Welsh Romance of Taliesin. Thirteenth century.

OLGER THE DANE

I. How Olger became Champion of France

Long ago, in the days when Denmark and England were almost like one country, the palace of the King of the Danes was dark and gloomy, and the sound of weeping and wailing rose within its walls; for the fair young queen, whom all the people loved, had died in giving birth to a son. When she was dead, they took the babe from her arms, and, having called him Olger, they carried him away to the royal nursery, and laid him on a quilted bed of down, and left him there alone. But ere long a sound of rustling was heard in the silent room, and there assembled round the bed six beautiful fairies, who smiled and kissed their hands to him; and the babe smiled back in return.

Then the Fairy Glorian took the child in her arms, and kissed him, and said: "My gift to you is that you shall be the strongest and bravest knight of all your time."

"And mine," said the Fairy Palestine, "is that you shall always have battles to fight."

"No man shall ever conquer you," promised the Fairy Pharamond.

"You shall ever be sweet and gentle," said Meliora.

And Pristina added: "You shall be dear to all women, and happy in your love."

Then Morgan le Fay, who was queen of all the fairies, took the boy in her arms, and pressed his head to her bosom, saying: "Sweet little one, there are few gifts for me to give you; but this shall be mine: You shall never die; and after you have lived a life of glory here you shall be mine, and shall dwell with me for ever in Avalon, the land of Faery." Then she kissed him many times, and laid him back upon the bed; and with soft rustling of wings the fays departed.

Ten years passed away, and Olger had grown a brave, strong boy, and comely to look upon.

At that time it befell that the Emperor Charles the Great sent a message to Godfrey, King of Denmark, and father of young Olger, to bid him come and do homage for his lands; to which King Godfrey, being a stout and stalwart man, made bold answer: "Tell Charles I hold my lands of God and of my good sword; and if he doubt it, let him come and see. Homage to him I will not do." So Charles the Great came up against him with a mighty army, and after long fighting King Godfrey was defeated, and forced to promise to appear before the Emperor every Easter to do allegiance. And, fearing lest he would not keep his word, the Emperor demanded that young Olger should be given to him as a hostage. To this King Godfrey agreed; and the boy was carried off to the Emperor's Court, and there instructed in all the arts and learning of the time, and so grew up an accomplished and handsome youth.

For three years King Godfrey appeared each Easter to do allegiance; but in the meantime he had married again. And when another son was born to him, his new wife persuaded him to cease to humble himself before the Emperor, for she hoped that by this means Olger would be put to death, and her own son would inherit the kingdom. So on the fourth Easter the King of Denmark appeared not at the Court; and so they took young Olger, and threw him into the prison of the Castle of St Omer, until messengers should find out why King Godfrey had broken his pledged word.

Now, the keeper of the castle was very good to the young man, who also found much favour in the eyes of his wife, and those of Bellisande, his daughter, who loved him from the first moment he appeared.

Instead of a gloomy dungeon Olger was placed in a rich apartment, hung with beautiful tapestry, and Bellisande herself was proud to wait upon him.

Meantime the messengers of Charles had met with a shameful reception at the hands of Godfrey, King of Denmark. Their ears and noses were slit, their heads shaven, and they were driven from the kingdom. Full of shame and wrath they appeared at the Court of their master, and cried loudly for revenge against Godfrey, and against his son Olger, since he stood as hostage for him. The Emperor at once gave orders that the lad should be put to death; but the keeper of the castle implored the Emperor not to insist upon instant execution, but at least to grant that the young knight should be brought before the Court and told why he must suffer death. To this the Emperor agreed; and as he sat at a great feast among his nobles there entered Olger, and kneeled meekly at his feet. When Charles saw how fair a youth he was, and how gently he humbled himself for his father's pride, he was moved with pity and compassion. Many of the nobles, too, were in favour of the lad, and would have begged the Emperor to save his life; but the rage of the messengers was so great that they would have torn him to pieces, had not Duke Naymes of Bayiere kept them back.

Then Olger looked up at the Emperor, and said:

"Sire, you know that I am innocent in this matter, and that I have always been obedient to you. Let me not suffer for my father's fault, but, since I am his true heir, let me pay the homage and allegiance which he refuses, and grant that I may atone for him by a life of devotion and service in your cause. And for your messengers, I will from this moment do all in my power to recompense them for the cruel indignities they have suffered at my father's hands, if you will but spare my life and use it in your service."

Then all the barons began to beg the King to grant the boy's request; and in the midst of the discussion a mounted knight rode into the hall, crying:

"Tidings, my lord King! Ill tidings for us all! The Soudan and the Grand Turk and Dannemont his son, with the help of King Caraheu, have taken Rome by storm, and Pope, cardinals, and all have fled. The churches are destroyed; the Christians put to the sword. Wherefore, as a Christian king and pillar of the Faith, I summon you to march to the aid of Holy Church."

Then, as all was bustle and confusion in preparing a great army to take the field immediately, Duke Naymes prevailed upon Charles to let him take young Olger to the battle as his squire, promising to give all his lands, and himself as prisoner, to the Emperor, if the boy should flee away. So Charles agreed, and hastened to prepare for the fight, swearing that he would not return to his own land till Rome should be restored to the Christians. The first thing Olger did when he recovered his freedom, was to hasten back to the castle and wed the fair Bellisande; and when she wept at losing her young husband so soon, he comforted her, and said: "Weep not, for God has given me life and you have given me love—and these two gifts will strengthen me to do great feats of arms."

So Olger rode off with the host, following the standard of Duke Naymes and his two brothers, Geoffrey and Gautier. And they marched till they came to Rome, and took their station on a hill before the city with an army of two hundred thousand men.

Then the host of paynims came forth from the city to the battle; and Olger, hearing the din of war, the neighing of horses, and the shouting of men, longed to dash into the thick of the fight; but his master forbade him, and charged him to remain among the tents.

From this position Olger watched with wild anxiety the standard of King Charles as it waved in the forefront of the battle. He saw the armies come together and heard a crash that rent the sky. Then the standard waved in triumph; but suddenly it fell—then rose again; and anon he saw with horror that the band of the Emperor's chosen knights had been repulsed, and that Sir Alory, the standard-bearer, had turned his horse, and was fleeing for his very life. In a moment Olger had rushed down the slope, and, flinging himself on the bridle of Sir Alory's horse, he snatched the standard from his hand, crying: "Coward, go home with all the speed you may, and live among women for the rest of your life, but leave the noble banner, Refuge of France, with me."

The terrified Alory was easily disarmed; and Olger, ordering a squire to dress him in the standard-bearer's armour, sprang on a horse and, sword in one hand and banner in the other, rushed into the thick of the fight.

He soon found that Duke Naymes and many other nobles had been held prisoners behind the array of the paynims, and, with the fierceness of a young lion, he cut his way through to them, freed their bonds with his sword, and forced a way through the enemy both for himself and for them. And wherever he appeared among the heathen host, he slew so many that he was protected, as it were, by a rampart of the dead. Presently he heard the King cry loudly for help, and, spurring in the direction of the sound, found that Dannemont had killed his horse under him, and that he was down, and hard pressed on every side. Then Olger, waving the standard on high, rushed upon the paynim, and soon cleared a free space about the King, and mounted him on a fresh horse. And in the same way on three separate occasions he saved the life of Charles. At length, with Olger at their head and the battle-cry of "Montjoy" on their lips, the King and his host drove the paynims back to the city gates.

When the fight was over, the Emperor Charles ordered the standard-bearer to be brought before him; and when Olger appeared, with his visor closed, he thought it had been Alory, and said to him: "Alory, though with grief I saw you flee at the onset, you have most nobly redeemed your honour. Three times have you saved my life, and I know not how to reward you fitly. I will make you ruler of any province you may choose in my kingdom, and you shall be my lieutenant, and fight in my quarrel in all disputes touching the crown of France."

But a squire who stood by spoke up, and said: "Sire, this is not that Alory of whom you speak. He bowed the colours, and fled for his life, at the first onset; but this young knight seized the standard from his hands, while I helped to dress him in Alory's armour; but who he is I know not."

Then Olger took off his helmet, and knelt down, and said: "Have pity, sire, on Godfrey, King of Denmark, and let his son atone for his offence and be your faithful vassal in his stead."

And the Emperor embraced him, and said: "You have changed all former hate into love for you. I give you your request. Rise, Sir Olger, Champion for France and Charles, and God be with you."

Thus Olger became a knight, and all the nobles of France came to salute him and thank him for their deliverance. On the next day, proud in his new-made knighthood, Olger once more bore the standard against the foe, and the paynims fell like corn before the scythe wherever he appeared. And when the Franks began to waver, then there rode into their midst a knight on a great horse, who did such mighty deeds on their behalf that they knew him for their Champion, and crying: "Olger! Olger the Dane!" they made many a mighty charge upon the foe.

When Sadonne, the paynim general, heard that the tide of battle was going against his army, he rode forth to meet his followers with the news that Cara-heu, Emperor of India, with thirty kings, was coming to their aid. But soon he met the whole array fleeing, panic-stricken, towards him in full flight, and crying, "Save yourselves, for Michael the Archangel fights against us!" Then, before Sadonne had time to flee, his path was crossed by the dread knight on the great horse, and at once he threw down his arms, and begged for life.

"What is your name?" said Sir Olger.

"I am Sadonne," answered he, "the general of Caraheu, Emperor of India."

"On one condition only will I grant you your life," said Sir Olger: "You must bear to Caraheu my challenge to fight with me in single combat, so that by this the course of the war may be determined."

So Sadonne departed, and next day Caraheu arrived at the pavilion of Charles the Emperor with a gorgeous retinue, and with him he brought the beautiful Gloriande, the fairest lady in all the Eastern world. Her hair was like spun gold, and fell to her feet like a cloak. It was bound about her temples by a jewelled circlet of the rarest gems, and her dress, of whitest damask sewn with pearls, had taken full nine years to weave.

Then Caraheu the Emperor said: "I am in search of Olger the Dane, who has demanded single combat with me. His challenge I accept, and fair Gloriande, my promised bride, shall be the victor's prize."

But Charlot, son of the Emperor Charles, looked with envy on Olger, and said: "'Tis meet that you, great Caraheu, should fight, not with my father's bondsman, but with me."

"Not I," replied the Emperor. "I fight not with braggarts, but with men. Sir Olger rules the hearts of men, which is nobler far than ruling over lands."

"Nay, Emperor," said Olger modestly; "Charlot here is the Emperor's son, and worthy to fight with the highest."

"Let him fight with Sadonne, my general," said Caraheu. "I will joust only with you."

So a double combat was arranged, and Gloriande sat in a place from which she could strengthen the combatants with the glances of her bright eyes. For half a day they fought without either getting the upper hand, until Sadonne killed Charlot's horse, and courteously leapt from his own in order to fight upon equal terms. But the base-minded Charlot only pretended to fight until he reached the place where Sadonne's steed was standing, and, leaping on it, he rode away, like a coward and recreant knight.

Meantime the good sword of Caraheu had cut through Sir Olger's shield and armour, and would have done worse harm had not the knight with his great strength dragged Caraheu from his horse, and disarmed him. But Dannemont, the paynim, had hidden three hundred men among the bushes of that place to see how the combat went. And when he saw Caraheu at Olger's mercy, he rushed forth at the head of his men, and began to attack the knight. In vain did Caraheu rail at them for their treachery, and fight with all his strength on Olger's side, crying: "Shame on ye, traitors! Better death than this!" Numbers overpowered them, and Olger's life was only saved at the request of the fair Gloriande. He was loaded with chains, and thrown into a dungeon, in spite of all that Caraheu could say or do on his behalf. At length, angry and disgusted at this foul blot on his honour, the latter left the paynim army, and went over with all his men to the side of the Emperor Charles, determined to go on fighting against the paynim until Olger was delivered. But Gloriande, who, according to the fairy gift, had loved Olger from the first moment she saw him, went in secret to his prison, loosed his chains, and let him escape to the camp of Charles. Then Charles and Olger and Caraheu joined together against the paynim host, and ere long Rome was freed from her enemies. Then Olger rescued Gloriande, and gave her to Caraheu to be his wife. In Rome were they baptised and married, and returned to India a Christian man and woman. But ere he departed, he gave to Olger his famous sword, Courtain, saying: "My life and my bride both have you won, and both you have given back to me; take, therefore, this sword as a pledge that I owe all to you."

II. The Vengeance of Olger

When Olger returned to France he found that his wife was dead. This grieved him very sorely, but he was comforted somewhat by the sight of the little son who had been born to him meantime. And he called his name Baldwin.

Now, at this time the paynims had come down upon Denmark, and had harried all the land. And they shut up King Godfrey in his own castle, and besieged it so that he nearly died of famine. Then the Queen said: "Surely this trouble is come upon us for Olger's sake, whom we left to die." And they began to repent of their wickedness, until at length, becoming very low and miserable, they sent a message to King Charles, begging him to forgive them, and to send them help. But the Emperor replied: "No! Since Godfrey holds his lands of God and of his good sword, let him hold them. I will not lift a hand to help him." Then he sent for Olger, and said: "You would not wish to help a traitor—one, too, who left you to die for his crimes?" But Olger knelt before the King, and said: "Sire, as vassal I kneel here before my King; but Godfrey is my father, and my duty is to go to his aid. Surely the King will not forbid a son his duty!"

Then Charles was moved, and said: "Go; but go alone, save with your body-servants. No man of mine shall fight in the cause of a rebel and traitor."

Then Olger hurried to his father's castle with thirty of his men; but ere he could reach it, King Godfrey had been slain by his foes, and they were even then fighting over his body when Olger rode up.

It was not long before Olger, with his good sword Courtain, had scattered these paynims far and wide, and soon after they left the country in despair of conquering such a hero. Then Olger was made King of Denmark, and ruled there for five years; and when he had settled the land and made good laws, he returned to the Emperor Charles, and, kneeling before him, said: "The son of Godfrey, of his own free will, thus pays homage to King Charles for all the land of Denmark."

The King embraced him warmly at these words, and begged him to remain as long as possible at the Frankish Court. Now, one day the little Baldwin, Olger's son, a fair-headed child whom all good men looked upon with favour, was playing chess with Charlot, son of the Emperor; and it came to pass that, having quickly given "fool's mate" to the prince, the boy began to laugh at him for his bad play.

Then Charlot, who had always hated Olger, and was jealous of young Baldwin, took up the heavy chessboard, and beat the child on the head, so that he fell lifeless to the ground.

When Olger returned from the hunt and found his little son lying dead, he was beside himself with grief. He covered the child with tears and kisses, and then, making his way to the Emperor's presence, he laid the boy before his throne, saying:

"Sire, look upon your son's foul deed."

The Emperor was sorely grieved; but he tried to comfort Olger, saying he would give half his kingdom if it would bring the child to life again, but that he knew well that nothing could make up for such a loss.

Then Olger said very sternly: "There is no compensation, but there is punishment to be given. Grant me now to fight with your son, and so avenge my poor child's death."

"Nay," said the Emperor; "for how, then, could he have a chance of life?"

"What matters that?" cried Olger, with bitter look. "What is your son more than mine? I demand that he be given up to me."

"I cannot do it," said the Emperor.

"Then," cried Olger in great wrath, "till you learn justice, sire, we part company." And forthwith he left the Court, and took service with a Lombard king who was fighting against King Charles.

For the next few years Olger the Dane won great renown by his warfare against the Franks, for wherever he went he was always the victor, and his enemies began to look upon his good sword Courtain, and Broiefort, his great black steed, with awe and terror. Many of the Franks said openly, that to let Olger depart and to make him their foe, had been no wise deed, for he came upon them like a blight upon the summer corn. At length they made a plot against him, and determined to get the better of him by foul treachery. So they watched him privily, and found him one day, tired out with fighting, lying fast asleep by a fountain, with his arms scattered far and wide, and his good steed Broiefort grazing peacefully by his side. Then one seized his horse, and another his weapons, and they bound him fast while he still lay sound asleep.

When Sir Olger was brought to the Court as a prisoner, the Emperor wished to slay him, because he feared the vengeance of Olger on his son, and in return for the harm he had done to the Frankish cause. But the knights and barons would not hear of this, saying that they had lent themselves to treachery to save their native land, but that the life of the noblest knight in Christendom should not be lost thereby. So he was put into prison, and kept under a strong guard for several years.

Now, after these days did Achar, King of England, land in France to do homage to the Emperor for his lands; and with him came his fair daughter Clarice. But as he journeyed to the Court a certain Saracen giant named Bruhier arrived with a great army to make war upon the Franks, and he seized the persons of Achar and his daughter, and marched to fight against the Emperor. And so great was the power of this giant that the Frankish army could not stand before him, but fled before his face. Then the barons and knights began to implore Charles to release Olger from his prison and prevail on him to fight for them, and forthwith the Emperor went himself ta the prison to implore his aid. But Olger would not listen for a moment to this proposal, unless the Emperor would first deliver Charlot the prince into his hands. For a long time the Emperor would not agree to this; but at length his whole army reproached him, saying: "Have you no care for us that you let us die by thousands in a hopeless fight? Why should a thousand die for one?"

So Charles was forced to deliver up his son.

Then, as Charlot begged and prayed for mercy, Olger thought only of his fair-haired little boy, and, taking the prince by the hair, raised Courtain to strike off his head. But as he did so a voice from the air cried: "Stay thy hand, Olger the Dane! Slay not the son of the King!" and at the same moment vivid flashes of lightning came about them both. Then the sword fell from Olger's hand, and all who had heard the voice trembled and greatly feared. The King, in his joy at the deliverance of his son, would have poured out his gratitude to the Dane; but Olger only said: "Your thanks are due to God, not to me. I do but bow to His will." And that day the King and Olger were made friends.

But when the Dane would have made ready to fight against the Saracen, he found that nothing had been heard or seen of his good horse Broiefort for seven long years, and all men believed him to be dead. The Emperor sent him his best charger in his stead, but scarcely had the knight leaped into the saddle when the creature fell beneath his weight. Ten other of the finest horses in the land were tried, and, finding that none could carry him, Olger declared that he must go afoot. But a certain man was found who said he had seen the horse Broiefort dragging blocks of stone for the building of the Abbey of St Meaux, and immediately a little band rode off to bring the horse back to his master. They found him but skin and bone, his hair worn off his sides, his tail shorn to the stump, his skin galled by the shafts, a very scarecrow of a horse, yet dragging a load that four other horses could not stir. They brought him to Olger with all speed; and when the sturdy knight leaned upon him, he did not cringe under the weight, but straightened himself, and, knowing his master, snorted and neighed with joy, and pawed the ground, and knelt down humbly before him on the grass.

So Olger went to battle upon Broiefort, and wherever he went he won the day. He slew the giant Bruhier, drove the Saracen from the land, and rescued King Achar, and his daughter Clarice, whom the King of Britain gave him for his wife. And when they were married, they crossed the sea, and Achar made Olger King of Britain in his stead. For many years he ruled this country, and there his faithful Broiefort died and was buried. At length he grew weary of peace, and went to fight for the Holy Cross in Palestine; and there he fought many a hard battle, and won many a victory, till he was old and grey with years. Then he left the Holy Land, and set sail for France that he might see

Charles the Great and his Court once more before he returned to Britain, there to end his days.

But on that journey there came upon them a great storm; and the tempestuous wind drove the ship in which Olger was far away from the rest, into strange seas, without rudder, oars, or mast; and a strong current seized the vessel, and crashed it against a reef of loadstone rock. All who were on board leaped into the waves, and were soon dashed lifeless against the beach; only Sir Olger remained upon the deck in the black darkness, gazing out upon the stormy sea. He bared his head, and, drawing Courtain, kissed the crossed hilt, and thanked God for the courage given him as a soldier all his life, and then quietly awaited death.

III. The Return from Avalon

Darker and wilder grew the night, when, just as the waves seemed about to overwhelm the ship, a voice from the air cried, clear and strong: "Olger, I wait for thee. Come, and fear not the waves." And immediately he cast himself into the sea, and was borne on the crest of a great billow high up in the air, and placed in safety among the rocks. A weird light shone through the gloom, and showed a narrow pathway through the crags, and, following this, Olger presently saw a brilliant glow in front of him, which gradually took the shape of a shining palace, which none can see by day, but which at nightfall glows with unearthly splendour. Its walls were of ivory, inlaid with gold and ebony, and within its spacious hall was set a most rare banquet upon a golden table. But the only inhabitant of the palace was a fairy horse named Papillon, who signed to Olger to seat himself at the banquet, and brought him water in a golden pitcher for his hands, and served him at table while he ate. When he had finished, Papillon carried him off to a bed, in the pillars of which stood golden candlesticks, wherein wax tapers burned the whole night through.

So Olger slept; but when he awoke next day, the fairy palace had vanished in the morning light, and he found himself lying in a fair garden, where the trees were always green and the flowers unfading and the summer never comes to an end, where no storm ever darkens the sweet, soft sky, and the chill of sunset is not known. For it was a garden in the vale of Avalon, in Fairyland.

And as he gazed around him, greatly wondering, there appeared at his side Morgan le Fay, Queen of the Fairies, clothed in shining white apparel, and said to him: "Welcome, dear knight, to Avalon. Long have I waited and wearied for your coming. Now you are mine for ever. The ages may roll away, and the world fall to pieces; we will dream for ever in this vale, where all things are the same." Then she put an enchanted ring on his finger, and immediately he became a youth again, beautiful and vigorous. And on his head she placed a crown of myrtle leaves and laurel, all in gold; and Olger remembered no more his former life, for she had given him the Crown of Forgetfulness.

So Olger sojourned in that fair land; and there he met and talked with King Arthur, healed now of his mortal wound, and the forms of Sir Lancelot and Sir Tristram and of many other noble knights of the Table Bound.

And so two hundred years passed by like a beautiful dream.

Meantime sad events had taken place in the land of France. No great leader had arisen after Charles the Great, and the land had fallen into poverty and shame. Everywhere the Franks were beaten back by Paynim and by Saracen, and chivalry seemed lost for ever. In vain the people cried out for a deliverer; and at length Morgan le Fay heard and pitied them. So she went to Olger the Dane, and said to him:

"Dear knight, how long have you dwelt here with me?"

"It may be a week, a month, or perchance a year," he answered, smiling, "for I have lost all count of time."

Then Morgan le Fay lifted the Crown of Forgetfulness from his brows, and at once his memory came to him again.

"I must go back," he cried, as though awaking from sleep. "Too long have I tarried here. Clarice will be calling for me, and Charles, my master, will have summoned Olger in vain. Where is my sword, my horse! Now let me go, fair queen, but tell me first how long I have dwelt here."

"It seems not long to me, dear knight," said she; "but you shall go when you will."

Then Morgan le Fay brought to life again his dead squire Benoist, and brought out Courtain, his good sword, and led forth Papillon for his steed. "Keep safe the ring upon your hand," said she, "for so long as you wear it, youth and vigour shall not fail you. And take also this torch, but see you light it not, for so long as it remains unlighted your life is safe; but, if ever it should begin to burn, guard the flame well, for with the last spark of the torch shall your days end."

She wove, moreover, a spell about them, so that they fell into a deep sleep. And when Sir Olger awoke, he found himself lying by a fountain, with his sword and armour near by, and Benoist holding Papillon ready for him to mount. Leaping on their horses, they rode along till, not far from a town, they overtook a horseman.

"What city is this, good sir?" asked Olger.

"Montpellier," answered the man.

"Ah, yes; I had forgotten," said Olger. "Yet I ought to know well enough, for a kinsman of mine is governor there." And he named the man whom he believed to be the governor.

"You are strangely in error," said the horseman, "though I remember now to have heard there was a ruler of that name two hundred years ago. He was a great writer of romances, and I daresay you know, since you claim him as your ancestor, that he wrote the romance of Olger the Dane. A good story enough, though, of course, no one believes it now, save perhaps one man, who often sings it about the city, and picks up money from the passers-by." Then he fell back a few paces, and riding beside Benoist, said to him: "Who is your master?"

"Surely you must know him," said the squire; "he is Olger the Dane."

"Rascal!" cried the stranger, "you are making a jest of me. All men know that Olger the Dane perished in shipwreck two hundred years ago. That is a fine story indeed!" And he rode away.

The knight and his squire pursued their journey till they came to the market-place of Meaux, where they stopped at the door of an inn well known to them in former days.

"Can we lodge here?" asked Olger.

"Certainly you can," replied the innkeeper.

"Then fetch the landlord to speak with me."

"Sir," said the man, "I am the landlord."

"Nay, nay," said Olger; "I wish to see Hubert the Neapolitan, the landlord of this house."

The man gave him one look, and then, taking him for a madman, bolted the door in his face, and, rushing to an upper window, cried: "Seize that horseman for a madman. He asks to see Hubert, my grandfather's grandfather, who has been dead two hundred years. Send for the Abbot of St Faron, that he may drive out the evil spirit from him."

Then a crowd began to gather, and stones and darts were hurled at the knight and his man, and in the scuffle that followed Benoist was shot dead by an archer. And when Sir Olger saw that, he was filled with the fiercest wrath, and rode Papillon at the crowd, and scattered them, cutting down with his sword all who came within reach. But so hotly burnt his wrath that it kindled the torch that he carried in his breast, so he rode away with it to the Abbey of St Faron. There the Abbot met him, to whom Olger said: "Is your name Simon? You at least should know me, seeing that I founded this abbey and endowed it with lands and money." But the Abbot answered that he knew little of those who had preceded him, and asked the stranger's name. And when he heard it he was greatly puzzled, and said to himself: "I do remember me that the charters of the house say that Simon was Abbot in the days of the founder, Olger the Dane; yet what does all this mean?" And aloud he said: "Sir Knight, the Abbot Simon has been buried for nigh two hundred years."

"What!" cried the knight. "Simon dead! And Charles the Great and Caraheu and Clarice, my wife? Where are they? Not dead too? Oh, say they are not dead!"

"Dead—dead two hundred years ago, my son," said the Abbot solemnly. Then Sir Olger was filled with awe and wonder, as he began to realise that his dream of Avalon was true after all. Following the Abbot into the church he told his strange story; and the Abbot believed him, and rejoiced to think that a deliverer had been sent to France at last. Then Olger told him the secret of the torch, and begged him to make an iron treasure-house beneath the church, wherein so little air could come that the flame might dwindle to a single spark, and yet be nourished and preserved for many years to come. And when this was done, and the torch was safely disposed of, the Abbot begged to see the magic ring. But when Olger heedlessly drew it from his finger, immediately his youth and vigour vanished, and he became a helpless old man, whose skin hung loose like withered parchment, and whose only sign of life was the quivering of his toothless jaws. The terrified Abbot hastily put back the ring on the fleshless finger, and immediately Olger's strength and youth returned, and he rode off on Papillon to fight for France. The enemy was then stationed before Chartres, and so strong they were that the Franks were falling back disheartened before them, when suddenly, just as in former days, a gigantic knight riding a coal-black horse appeared in their midst, and everywhere he rode was marked by a long line of slain. Then the astonished Franks remembered the stories they had heard in the days of old, and murmured to one another: "It is Olger the Dane!" One after the other passed it on, till the murmur grew to a cry, and the cry to a shout of "Olger! Olger the Dane!" and, rushing upon the foe, they swept the paynims from the field. Over and over again did Olger thus lead the Franks to victory, until at length the land was free. And always while he fought the torch burned bright in the Church of St Faron, but when he rested it dwindled to a spark again.

At length the renowned and glorious knight had leisure to visit the French Court. He found that the King of France had lately died, but the Queen received him with all kindness; and her waiting maid, the Lady of Senlis, loved him so much that she would gladly have wedded him, but he would have nothing to do with her. Now, one day these ladies discovered the secret of the magic ring; for, finding him one day asleep upon a couch after a long journey, they drew the ring from his finger, meaning to jest with him about it when he awoke. Much to their horror, the strong man withered up before their eyes, and became an ancient skeleton. Then the Queen, knowing from this that it was truly Olger the Dane, immediately replaced the ring, and he regained his former youth. But the Lady of Senlis, determined that since Olger did not care for her, he should love no one else, sent thirty strong knights to waylay him as he left the Court, and to wrest the ring of Morgan le Fay from his hand. But Sir Olger spurred Papillon among them, with Courtain drawn in his hand, and so escaped untouched. After this the Queen herself wished to marry Olger, for she said: "He, and he alone, is worthy to sit upon the throne of Charles the Great." And to this Olger agreed, for he felt to sit in his master's seat was the highest earthly honour he could win. So with great pomp and ceremony they prepared for the wedding. The great church blazed with golden banners as a lordly procession entered and proclaimed the approaching coronation of the new-made King; and Sir Olger took the Queen by the hand, and led her forward, and knelt with her upon the chancel pavement. But ere the marriage vows were spoken, a brighter light than any on earth shone upon them, and all at once a thick white cloud wrapped round the knight. Some say that Morgan le Fay was seen floating down through the cloud, with arms outstretched, to carry off her knight. However that may be, when the cloud had cleared away Sir Olger was no more to be seen upon this earth. But men whisper that Olger the Dane lives yet, for the torch still burns in the treasure-house of the Abbey of St Faron. He is only asleep in the faery islands of Avalon, and one day he will awaken, and return again, return to deliver France once more in time of need, when the Franks shall turn, and conquer their foes, with their ancient battle-cry of "Olger! Olger the Dane!"

From the Anglo-Norman Romance of Charlemagne, about the twelfth century, but undoubtedly borrowed from a Celtic source, since the whole spirit of the tale is Celtic in origin.

THE STORY OF KING FORTAGER

Constaunce, King of Britain, was a mighty man of valour, and in his days the people were freed from their enemies, but when he died, his eldest son, Moyne the Monk, who had lived all his days in the Abbey of Winchester, sat upon the throne. Now when Angys the Dane saw King Moyne to be but a studious youth, hating the thought of warfare, he gathered an army together, and sailed for Britain.

Then was there great terror in the land; and King Moyne gave orders to Fortager, his father's steward, that he should put himself at the head of the Britons, and fight against Angys. But Fortager pretended to be very sick, so that he could not go forth to battle. Then King Moyne was obliged to go himself, and so badly did he conduct the fight that the Britons were defeated. And Angys took many British towns and castles, and fortified them against their former owners. Now, there had fought under King Moyne twelve British chieftains who were very ill content with the state of affairs. They came together, and said: "If Fortager had been our leader this would not have happened so." Then they went to Fortager to ask his counsel. But Fortager would only say: "Seek counsel of your King; it will be time enough to ask for mine when Moyne is King no longer."

On hearing these words, the twelve chieftains went straightway to King Moyne, and slew him as he sat at meat within his hall; after which they returned to Fortager, and greeted him as King. But there were many who yet loved the race of good King Constaunce, and some of the barons took his two young sons, Aurilis-Brosias and Uther-Pendragon, the brothers of King Moyne, and sent them away to Brittany, lest they too should be slain.

Meantime Fortager had called together a great army, and had fought with Angys and driven him from the land; and he would have killed the Dane as he prepared to flee, had not Angys begged for mercy and promised to make war no more on Britain.

So Angys sailed away with his host, and Fortager marched in triumph to the capital. And while he was feasting in the palace, the twelve chieftains who had slain King Moyne came to him, and said: "O King, remember it was we who made you King and placed you here on high; give us now a reward." And Fortager answered: "Now that I am King I will indeed give a meet reward for traitors." And, having ordered wild horses to be brought in, he watched them tear the traitors limb from limb upon his castle pavement. Now, by this deed Fortager roused the wrath of all who had helped him to his throne, and many spoke of bringing back Aurilis-Brosias and Uther-Pendragon to the land. And Fortager was hunted through the kingdom, and sorely beaten, so that he scarce escaped with his life.

At length he determined to send for help to King Angys, which he forthwith did, promising him half the kingdom if he would come to his aid. So Angys returned again with many men and ships, and by his aid Britain was subdued by force of arms. But though the war ceased there was no peace in the land; and Fortager went about in deadly fear, first of the Britons whom he had betrayed, and next of Angys, lest with his powerful host he should seize the whole kingdom. And lastly, he feared that the men of Brittany would come over and fight for Aurilis-Brosias and Uther-Pendragon, and bring them back to their father's throne.

So he determined to build a strong castle, made of well-hewn stone and timber—an impregnable fortress with lofty towers and battlements, a deep moat and heavy drawbridge—such as had never been seen for strength in the world before; and he decided to rear it on Salisbury Plain, and so be surrounded by wastes of land, and far from his foes. At daybreak three thousand men began the work—hewers of wood and carpenters and masons and cunning workers in stone. The foundations were laid deep, on vast blocks of stone clamped with iron; and by nightfall the wall had risen breast-high. But when they came to their work next morning, they found to their dismay that the ground was scattered with the stones they had built up, and that all they had done was destroyed. That day they built it up again, laying the foundations deeper than before, and clamping each stone to the next with iron. But when they came next morning all was overthrown as before.

Then Fortager called together ten wise men, and shut them in a tower, open to the sky, that they might read the stars, and find out why these things should be. And after nine days the wise men came to him, and said:

"Sire, we read in the stars that an elf child has been born in Britain, knowing things past and things to come. Find the child, and slay him on this plain, and mix the mortar with his blood, and so shall the wall stand fast." So Fortager sent men forth to journey far and wide till they should find the child, and after wandering for many days and weeks, one party of messengers came to a certain town, and found some children quarrelling in the market-place at their games.

"Thou son of a black elf," they heard one say, "we will not play with thee, for we know not who thou art." The messengers gazed hard at the five-year-old child thus addressed; and immediately the boy, who was called Merlin, ran up to them, and said: "Welcome, O messengers, and behold him whom you seek. But think not, for all men may say, that my blood will ever make firm the castle walls of Fortager; for his wise men who try to read the stars are but blind, and they blunder past what lies at their very feet."

Then the men wondered greatly, and said: "How didst thou know of our errand?"

And Merlin answered: "I can see as it were pictures of all that is and all that shall be. I will go with you to Fortager, and show what hinders building up his fortress on the Plain."

So he mounted a pony, and followed after the men on horseback.

And as they journeyed through a town, they saw a man buying strong new shoes and leather wherewith to mend them when they wore out; and Merlin laughed to himself.

"Why do you laugh?" asked the messengers.

"Because he will never wear the shoes," replied the boy. And so it came to pass, for the man fell dead at his door as he carried home the shoes.

And next day Merlin laughed again, and, being asked why, said: "King Fortager is jealous because his Queen's chamberlain is better looking than he, and he threatens to take his life, knowing not that the handsome fellow is but a woman in disguise."

And when they came to the palace, they found that it was just as the boy had said, so the chamberlain's life was spared. Then Fortager marvelled greatly at the wisdom of this child of five years, and begged him to reveal the mystery of his castle wall. And Merlin said: "The fiends have deceived your wise men by showing false signs among the stars; for my kindred of the air are very wroth because I have been baptised into Christendom, and they seek to destroy my life. But if you send your men to dig a yard beneath the wall's foundation, they will there find a stream of water running over two

mighty stones, under which live two dragons. Each night at sundown these dragons wake, and do battle, so that the earth is shaken, and the wall falls down."

Then Fortager set his men to dig beneath the foundations as Merlin had said; and presently they came to a fast and furious stream, which they turned off by making another channel. And in the river-bed were two huge stones, which it took many men to heave up, and there beneath them lay the dragons. One was as red as fire, and his body a rood in length, with eyes that gleamed like red-hot coals, and a strong and supple tail. The other was milk-white, and very grim of look; he had two heads, and darted out white fire from his jaws. And at sight of them, as they awoke from slumber, all save Merlin fled in panic. Then the dragons arose, and began to fight. And soon the air was full of the fiery breath from their throats, so that it was like lightning on the earth, and the whole land shook with their noise and fury. All that long summer night they fought with tooth and nail and claw, and fell and rose, and fell and rose again, till the day dawned. And by that time the red dragon had driven the white into a valley, where for a while the latter stood at bay; but at length, recovering himself, he forced the red dragon back into the plain again, and, fixing his claws in his throat, tore him to pieces, and with his fiery flame scorched him up to a heap of ashes on the plain. Then the white dragon flew away into the air.

From that time Merlin became a great favourite of King Fortager, and counselled him in all things. And now, when the masons began to build, the wall no longer fell down as before, and in course of time a fair white castle arose upon the plain, stronger and mightier than any that the world had ever seen.

Then Fortager sent for Merlin, and asked what the battle of the dragons really meant, and if it betokened things that should yet come to pass. But the boy would answer nothing. Then in his anger King Fortager threatened to slay him; but Merlin only laughed in scorn, saying:

"You will never see my death-day. Strike if you will, and bind me fast, but you will only fight the air."

Then Fortager began to entreat him humbly, and swore that no harm should come to him whatever he should say. And at length Merlin told him that the red dragon betokened Fortager and the power he had obtained through killing King Moyne. The white dragon with the two heads represented the true heirs, Aurilis-Brosias and Uther-Pendragon, whose kingdom he held, and as the white dragon, hunted to the valley, there regained his breath, and drove back the red dragon to the plain, so should these heirs, driven out to Brittany, find help and succour there, and were even now sailing to Britain with a vast army to hunt King Fortager through the land, and to drive him to his castle on the Plain. And there, while he was shut up, with his wife and children, he should be burnt to ashes.

Then King Fortager, when he heard this, was grieved at heart, and prayed Merlin to tell him how to avoid this terrible fate, or at least how he might escape with his life. But Merlin only answered:

"What will be, will be."

Then Fortager, in his wrath, tried to seize the boy; but Merlin vanished from his sight, and while they sought him, he was all the time far away in the cell of Blaise the hermit. And there he remained for many a year, and wrote a book concerning all the things that were going to happen in Britain.

Meantime all that he had foretold took place. For Uther-Pendragon and his brother marched to Winchester with an army, and when the citizens saw the banner of their old British kings, they drove out the Danish garrison, and opened the gates to the sons of Constaunce. And not one of the men of Britain would fight on the side of Fortager or Angys, nor would the men of their armies fight against their friends and brothers in the land. So they won an easy victory, and drove Fortager away to his fortress on Salisbury Plain, where he shut himself up with his wife and children. And the men of Britain threw wild-fire on the walls, and burnt him there, and all that belonged to him, and made his castle walls level with the ground.

But Angys fled away to a fortress on a hill, whither Uther-Pendragon followed, but could not come to him because of the strong bulwarks by which it was surrounded.

Then, hearing men speak often of the wisdom of Merlin, Uther-Pendragon sent men far and wide to seek him. And one day, when these messengers sat at dinner, there came in to them an old beggar, with a snow-white beard and ragged shoes and a staff in his hand, and said: "Ye are wise messengers who seek the child Merlin! Often to-day have ye passed him on the road, and yet ye knew him not. Go back to Uther, and tell him that Merlin waits in the wood hard by; for, search as ye will, ye will never find him."

And with these words the old man disappeared. Then the messengers, wondering greatly, returned, and told all to Uther, who left his brother to maintain the siege, and went to the wood to seek Merlin. And first he met a swine-herd, who said he had lately seen the elf child, and then a chapman with his pack, who said the same. Then came a countryman, who said that Merlin would surely keep his tryst, but that Uther must be patient, as he still had some work to do ere he sought the palace.

So the prince waited patiently far into the night; and at length the countryman returned to him, saying: "I am Merlin, and I will now go with you to the camp."

When they got there Aurilis-Brosias came out to meet them, and said: "Brother, there came a countryman in the night, who waked me, saying: 'Angys is come out of his fortress, and has stolen past your sentinels, and is in your camp, seeking to take your life.' So I sprang up, and, seeing Angys at the door, I rushed upon him, and slew him, my sword passing through his coat of mail as if it had been naught. But when all was over, the countryman had vanished."

Then Uther answered: "Brother, here is the countryman, and he is Merlin." Then were the princes much rejoiced, and thanked Merlin for his timely aid. And in the morning the Danes and Saxons yielded up their citadel, and asked leave to sail away to their own land.

So the country was once more free; and the Britons took Uther-Pendragon, the elder of the brothers, and crowned him King at Winchester.

For seven long years he reigned and prospered; and Merlin was counsellor not only to him, but to his son, the great King Arthur, after him.

Amongst the deeds which were performed by the magician to please the King, it is told:

"How Merlin, by his skill, and magic's wondrous might,

From Ireland hither brought the Stonendge in a night."

DRAYTON.

And many of these stones may still be seen standing upon Salisbury Plain. From the Romance of Merlin. Thirteenth or fourteenth century.